THE RIDE TO WORK

THE RIDE TO WORK

CR PAGE

Turn the Page Creations

This book is published by Turn the Page Creations

Fullarton SA 5063 Australia

Copyright © 2022 CR Page

Cover designed and created by Alison Page Photography

A catalogue record for this book is available from the National Library of Australia

ISBN 978-0-6454757-0-8 (Paperback)
ISBN 978-0-6454757-1-5 (E-Book)

First published 2022

For Alison, whose constant belief and support made this possible.

CHAPTER 1

MONDAY MAY 16, 2022

8.20am

Monday morning. The words conjure depressing images like no other point of the week. You don't need to be a nine-to-five worker to understand the meaning. The Monday morning feeling exists for everyone, even if it isn't in these hours. As life has crushed me further, I retain the Monday morning feeling all week. Today, though no better, the feeling is very different. It was the last time I would face this routine. I'd like to say that I had found a better alternative, but there is nothing better about it. Sometimes different is as good as it gets.

From the moment I close the door behind me, it will be thirty-two minutes until I clock-in. For seven years I have ridden my bicycle along the same streets, from my inner-suburban home to my central city workplace. It is a well refined routine. A head wind, or a poor run of red lights may push this out marginally, but I can take it for granted that if

I can leave in the next minute, I will swipe my identification card to clock-on at 8.53am. I have a meeting with Sam, the manager of the branch, at 9am. I would have appreciated a little extra time to psychologically prepare at my desk, but I will be too late for that. At least I would not be making Sam wait, which was fortunate. Patience is rarely the strength of managers, and in our branch that is especially true. Now that I think of it, I am not sure what Sam's strengths are.

I still have not shut the door. Despite being virtually ready at 8am, I keep remembering something else. My ID card, then my keys. Surely now I've got everything. By the end of the day nothing is going to matter, but I am too much a creature of habit to think of things in this way. No doubt the emotions running through me are heightened this morning. I want no complications and am doing my best to make the commute as much like every other day as possible. Shit, the stereo is still on. With my eclectic tastes, INXS, Nirvana, and Crowded House amongst others have been playing on loop all morning.

I remember once telling my colleague Rob that he could tell my mood from my appearance. When I was well presented, it was a sign that I was in a good place mentally. The scruffier I looked, the more it showed that life was swamping me. This wasn't entirely true. I tended to make an effort to start each week looking presentable, however much the Monday morning feeling dominated me. As the week went by, my appearance tended to deteriorate in a linear fashion. When I already looked a mess on Monday, it didn't bode well.

I lowered my tall, slender frame to examine myself in the mirror. The lines on my face formed a roadmap telling more of how I had lived than the length of time. I'm forty-six, though I doubt anyone would guess below fifty, the greying hair adding a few more years to my look.

I would clearly fail Rob's presentation test today, not that he'll be there to notice thanks to a rostered day off. Actually, it is his absence that has led me to plan my day the way I have. He is the property manager, and acts as a liaison between our department and the building owner. He has the master keys to every part of the building. In his absence I can get a hold of these, and I will need them later this morning. I don't work in the same area and shouldn't be aware of where to find them. Luckily, after enough drinks one night, he gave me an access code, supposedly under the guise of it being available in case of emergency. Naturally if such an emergency occurred, it would not fall on a staff member from another part of the building to deal with it. There was no justification for his divulgence, but I had decided to retain that information for any personal emergency I may have. I was ready to nominate today as such an emergency. I have never used it before. It has always been evident that I could not use the code without later being reprimanded severely for it. Any use is recorded and there was no way I would be able to vindicate the use of keys that I am not entitled to access. It would be treated, quite simply, as theft. Once punishment becomes irrelevant, this no longer feels like a threat. Today I can act without fear. Subtlety and timing are all I need.

Home is such a mess. It frustrates me, but seemingly not enough. The time I spend bemoaning the state of my home could be spent doing something about it. If I did, then the problem wouldn't exist. It is an example of momentum dictating results. If you do nothing, things deteriorate. Once they are bad enough it becomes more difficult to begin. I find examples of that from many distinct aspects of life. Anything destructive I seem quick to begin, then make continual progress. Anything that offers a positive way forward seems like something that I constantly plan yet never commence. If only I could begin, maybe momentum would ensure that I'd be able to make more of life. That is in no way an excuse, for it is only within me that the solution has ever existed. Many people struggle to differentiate, but there is a substantial difference between a reason and an excuse.

I was born in Adelaide in 1975 and have spent most of my life here. In my early thirties I followed what I thought was the love of my life and moved to the Gold Coast. I was there for five years before moving back a changed man in 2012. I bought the unit I live in two years later and have lived here alone ever since. When I bought here, I had my father in the next suburb, but he died a couple of years later. My only surviving family are scattered, with my mother in Brisbane, sister in Tasmania and brother in London. My contact with each of them is minimal. Mum and Vanessa visited when I had major surgery last year, but that aside there has been nothing more than a yearly birthday card. I pushed them away for decades, but it has only been the last couple of years when the relationships have truly crumbled. What will they think when they hear what happens? Will it impact them?

It is a lonely existence for me here, despite being the original hometown of our family. When circumstances brought me back to Adelaide, I knew this could end up being the case, but it always had felt like home to me. I never loved my old hometown, but it had felt like a security blanket for me. I'd constantly alienated people on my descent, so such a feeling wasn't likely to come from others. New relationships could happen anywhere, but I was just as likely to drive these people away before long.

What do I have to look forward to? I am not sure how most people answer that question, though I suspect in many cases there are references to the people they love. When you have lost those people, or at least the certainty of their love, it dramatically reduces the ability to look forward enthusiastically. I find it impossible to manufacture enthusiasm, so without something inspiring my view of the future, I am left to look forward bleakly.

I used to have passions, but one by one it has been harder to retain the same feelings for these things. As your enthusiasm for life diminishes, how can you still be as keen about the pastimes that used to mean so much to you. Life was fuelled by my love of animals, books, cooking, music, and art. I hungered to learn more, see more and experience more. Eventually I reached a point in life where the hunger disappeared. Moments that had previously brought excitement began to feel hollow. Emptiness seemed omnipresent. I can't pinpoint a moment when life turned this way. Through tragedy and disaster there always seemed a light within me that could be turned on, even if it became dimmer over the years. Now the light seems permanently out.

I loved to cook. I should have become a chef, but it was my weekend passion back in the days when I had people to cook for. I earned the nickname Bourdain for my culinary expertise though the fact it still gets used these days is more in recognition of my love of travel. This had been another passion, but one that ended not through my state of mind, but the global pandemic. The result was the same. An absence of anything to look forward to.

I used to believe in things. Politics, environmental and human rights issues. Both locally and globally I sought to help bring change. Doing what we could to make the world a better place. My beliefs haven't changed, but I no longer see the point towards pursuing the goals. However hard you strive, you are always fighting a system that is designed to beat you. Humanity has fought for action on climate change for decades, but what have we achieved? There are too many vested interests with too much to lose and they retain their hold. Even if we finally make progress, what is the point for me? There is no future generation of my family to benefit. I know it sounds selfish, but that is reality. To some degree selfishness drives all living creatures. Once there is no gain to us or our genes things don't hold the same importance.

Weekends usually fly, but not this one. I dreaded anyone asking what I had gotten up to, as since I rode home on Friday, I cannot detail one thing I've done. Sure, I ate, I showered, I shat, but that's hardly a set of achievements to tell the world about. To be fair it seemed like an achievement to do those things with where my mind was at. There is no task so sufficiently simple that a depressed person can take it for granted.

I did not go to bed last night. My mind was in no place for sleep, so I just stayed up. In the middle of the night I decided to read a book. Needing something both familiar and short, I settled on Hemmingway's *"The Old Man and the Sea."* I found myself relating all too closely to Santiago as he faces the collapse of his dream. Admittedly, I didn't have the same legitimacy to a claim on glory as the fisherman.

My life is a lie. I do not try and present false truths to people, but I do keep what is genuine close to my chest. Through all the dramas I've lived, those that have had glimpses of what's beneath have emphasised the need for me to talk, but I've never been comfortable with that. Living in a realm of self-hatred isn't easy, but if it allows a modicum of respect from others then there is some reason to live. Most people's reason to live is for the love of others. When you lack that, you need to hang on to anything you can find that gets you through.

Sometimes I see suffering, genuine suffering, and I reflect on my life with even greater self-hatred. How can I feel so wronged by life that I want it to end when people overcome the most severe physical and mental disabilities yet find the will to survive? The truth is that whatever you do or don't have, so long as you possess some degree of hope, there is nothing you cannot conquer. I remember hope as on old friend that always promised more than she delivered. One day she was nothing more than a memory, and from that time on I've been going through the motions without any under-standing of why. Wasn't it inevitable that one day I would be able to take it no more?

I feel like I'm trapped in a hole that has been dug spe-cifically for me over the past four decades. The first soil was turned by the universe itself before people that came into my life took the shovel and started digging. As the years passed and I found myself losing sight of what life should be from inside the hole, I became the one doing most of the digging.

Progressively life got darker as I found myself living deeper below the surface. Years ago, I realised I could not find a way out. Still, I continued to dig, and to this day find myself getting even further from the light.

Just another bicycle commute for just another day at work. That is how it may look, though appearances often deceive. The ride to work may be like every other day, but what will follow could not be any further from regular. Nobody else knows it yet, but everyone will remember today. I keep wondering just what impact the day will have on other people. Maybe some will over analyse it and their own role leading up to it. Maybe the people I would most want to re-evaluate themselves will ignore it. In saying that, it is not about anyone else. My decisions are about me. I have been led to them by a myriad of events over 40 years. It is like I have climbed a hundred steps up a staircase to reach this point. Those who only saw me on the last few steps could do nothing to change my trajectory. Nevertheless, the attitude of a couple of those people was such that I wanted them to see the consequences. They may not care, but they were damn well going to know all about it.

CHAPTER 2

Finally I close the back door behind me and step out into the day. Shit, my estimated time of arrival is now back to 8.54am. I am cutting things even finer.

The weather couldn't be more perfect. Overcast and cool but no sign of rain. Most people would have said Saturday was ideal with its blue sky and warmth, but I don't enjoy the sun. Perhaps the brightness provides too much contrast with how I feel and exacerbates my emotions. A darker day allows my mood to blend in. It is also far more comfortable when riding to work in these cooler conditions. I ride in on the forty degree days in the summer and on days where it is pouring with rain. In both cases, I shower at work and the comparative time savings of riding in are lost. In conditions like todays, I can ride in perfect comfort, not raising a sweat on the way in, and I am ready to start work just a minute or two after arriving at the building.

Sam probably expects me to call in sick today to avoid the confrontation. Given my track record, that expectation shouldn't exist. While many of our staff seem to be absent following the slightest workplace issue, my presence could be relied upon however bad things were. Whatever the issues may be, I have always been willing to face the consequences while others have sought to hide from them. Willing may not be the appropriate word, but I'd inflicted enough damage on myself at times that my available absences had been blown on recovery. There was nothing else to spare.

Sam caught me just as I was leaving on Friday. Knowing I couldn't be kept there at that time, today's meeting was organised. I'd had a major run-in with Terry earlier in the day. When I saw him in Sam's office for an extended period in the afternoon, I knew that I was the topic. I am adamant that I did and said nothing wrong, but of course Sam will have heard his version of the story rather than the truth. Terry may not have lied, but everyone interprets things in their own way. As sure as I referred to the overcast conditions this morning as perfect, someone else may call it an ugly grey day. We'd both be giving an accurate account but only within our perspective. Terry and I certainly see most things within the workplace in quite opposite ways.

In my role as a team leader, I supervise staff. Our branch is evenly split between those who seem like they have been here forever, and the latest array of so-called talent to come through the revolving door. I report to a section manager, and for a while that was Terry. Circumstances between us were never good, and the decision was made to move me under Madeleine's management.

Sam arrived at the branch three years ago, following the previous manager departing for a new job. Most of us had expected his replacement to be either Terry or Madeleine, his two deputies. This was both our great fear, and our great hope. Terry is the most destructive force imaginable in an office environment, while Madeleine is a dream to work with. When the decision was announced that an outsider had won the role, we felt like sports fans when their team draws a match; the horror result had been avoided yet you couldn't celebrate the victory you'd been hoping for.

The public sector is small enough that there is only a couple of degrees of separation. Information and opinions about Samantha Sorrell were flowing constantly, but there appeared to be two vastly differing perspectives. While people seemed quick to believe one or the other, I remained cautious of opinion. Nobody is universally admired nor hated. Even Terry has fans. Even Madeleine has critics. Neither of these seem understandable to most people who have worked with them, but it is testament to the different outlooks we all have. In the time Sam has been here, I have seen plenty of examples that justify each of the popular opinions about her. My over-riding feelings may be negative, but I'm realistic enough to see certain aspects she excels in, even if they are elements that I consider unsuitable for this particular workplace.

Radical change followed by an eventual realisation that nothing is different. Common wisdom teaches us not to fix what isn't broken. This does not suit new managers. Team success is pointless unless their fingerprints are deeply embedded. All achievements should connect to their personal legacy. If the best approach is the current one, it must first be destroyed with a scapegoat blamed, before a rebuild with their signature attached. With the sleight of hand to make a magician proud, they stand centre stage awaiting the standing ovation that is not shared. The audience marvels at the change, oblivious to the fact that no real change has occurred.

Sam mastered this approach. Terry had been frustrated by losing out to her and wanted to move upward and out. Under the promise of enhanced opportunities, he played the role Sam wanted, tearing the fabric of the branch apart for six months before being parachuted into a year-long opportunity elsewhere in the department. When he left, he carried the blame for all that Sam had enacted. From that point in time the second part of Sam's plan began. To all with a decent memory, the end product was indistinguishable from what we had previously known.

For the twelve months Terry was gone, I acted in his role as a section manager. The change from being a team leader to a section manager was substantial. I had been used to the occasional meeting, but most of my time had normally been direct assistance and guidance of my staff. In the management position, I had little direct dealings with staff. I was constantly in meetings, be it with Sam and Madeleine at a management level, or with the three team leaders who were now reporting to me. I was less enthused with the nature of this role, but it was a valuable learning experience.

I got to know Sam well in this period. I sat in regular meetings; one-on-one, as a trio with Madeleine, as well as part of bigger committees. Like a politician, she had the ability to present a caring and personable quality to all. Behind closed doors, she never held back on her opinions of various staff members. Not only would she talk down their relevant capabilities, but she also made cutting, personalised comments that reflected worse on her than the people she denigrated. She showed blatant favouritism to those who fitted her personal preferences. Well-presented young people flourished, irrespective of the incompetence they showed. If they showed any enthusiasm in conversation with her, she took them under her wing and sought to push them beyond their potential. They could be lazy, ignorant and unintelligent, but it never held them back. Wear the wrong shoes and that was another story. She wrote off anyone who'd been in our workplace for longer than five years, irrespective of their strengths. It was so obvious, yet whenever complaints were raised with the human resources department, enquires ended before they began. I wasn't sure if it was cynicism or insightfulness on my part, but I was certain that she had some sort of hold over people at the highest levels. She seemed to be able to operate without any restrictions.

Sam did have many innovative ideas about advancing the branch, and working with her and Madeleine, I believed we were achieving positives on a greater level that offset her great failings. When Terry's twelve-month absence was ending, Sam was keen to create a new role on the management team to utilise my strengths. I was less enthused; working closely with Sam and Madeleine was one thing but adding Terry to the mix was not going to have the same level of cohesiveness. I explained this to Sam and reverted to my previous team leader level. Whether it was done as punishment or not, I was moved to a different team than I'd previously been in. I would now have Terry as my section manager. I'd gone against her wishes and I was immediately added to her hit-list.

I didn't care enough about the workplace to lose sleep about the decisions, but I hated the change in atmosphere that had occurred. Terry's intensity meant that nobody could breathe and relax at any point. There was always a new issue. Always something that needed attention. Always someone who had to pay a price.

Terry and I had long had a strange relationship. With Madeleine and Patrick, he had interviewed me when I first came to the branch. He was my team leader, albeit briefly, several years ago. I had found him incredibly difficult to deal with. He organised rosters for staff that were based around his friendships. He set strict policies on key performance indicators, but only enforced them on certain people. He developed close personal relationships with staff, and those who he had an involvement with outside of work tended to have a vastly better experience in the office. It wasn't a secret, but it all seemed too difficult for management to do anything about it.

Several years later we'd had management changes and a restructure. Terry and Madeleine advanced from team leaders to section managers. I moved into one of the team leader roles that had been vacated. Working under Madeleine had been a delight, but under Terry it was a nightmare. It had only been a brief period that we worked together, in these roles, but it brought back the problems I'd had when he'd first been my team leader. When he came back after the twelve month secondment, he was more unhappy than ever. The dynamic between us was destructive from the beginning. It only took a couple of months before Sam accepted that it couldn't work.

'Bloody hell. You don't deserve this, but it's just too much bloody trouble to do it any other way,' she told me.

'You know what he's like Sam, and you know what I'm like. Who do you really think the problem is?' I asked.

'Both of you. You need to be professional enough to work with whoever your manager is, and whoever you manage. He may be difficult, but you're not that easy either.'

Terry wanted Sam's job. He'd wanted it before she arrived and hadn't lost sight of that aim since. He didn't care whether he got her out of the door through a promotional opportunity or through creating trouble for her, so he seemed to try both methods. Sam was aware of his nature, and when I'd been her confidante as a section manager, she'd never sought to keep that a secret. As though she believed my memory had been wiped when reverting to my substantive role, she felt she could now convince me that she bore no ill feelings towards him.

The politics of the workplace is a reality for most people. I don't know that ours is inherently worse than most. I think the mix is not abnormal. Madeleine and Terry, like night and day, falling under Sam who shared some of the best and worst characteristics of each of them. A range of team leaders underneath these who varied from the ambitious to the incompetent and the jaded. At every level beneath were examples of the same, but I venture to say that similar attributes would be evident in most other workplaces.

Why I am going through all of this shit this morning is beyond me. I'm not paid enough to bring workplace issues home with me, but I can't help it. It's bugged me enough over the weekend, it's hard to see how it wouldn't be on my mind now. The ride home is often dominated by thoughts of the day just passed, but usually I can avoid it in the morning.

My bike leans against the wall. It was semi-protected from the elements, still being treated with care having only been in my possession for a week. My previous bike was stolen from the local shopping centre. Bastards. As I walk towards it, I commit to casting Terry out of my thoughts. Sometimes these things are easier said than done, and I know I may end up stewing on Friday's fight the whole journey. I always have an over-active mind when I'm on the bike, so it's just as likely that my mind will deviate several times along the ride. The trek is always quicker and easier when my focus is less on pedalling and more on virtual conversations or the making of plans in my head.

I unstrap my helmet from its resting place attached to the frame of the bike. I put it on my head and walk the bike towards the gate. I take a last look at the backyard and close the gate behind me. After a deep breath of contemplation at what lays ahead, I put my left foot on the pedal and push off, throwing my right leg over the frame and positioning that foot onto the other pedal. The bike begins to transport me from my carport towards the shared driveway of the group of units, and finally I am on my way.

Better late than never. Actually, never would have been much better.

CHAPTER 3

8.24am

Australian cities are behind most European and Asian cities for the volume of bicycles on the road. Of eighty people in my office, I know of only two others who cycle to work. My relative lack of fitness means I need the exercise, but that is a benefit rather than a reason. It is far cheaper than driving or public transport, but again this isn't the reason. It also is the quickest way of me getting to work. Traffic congestion and the distance of the nearest car park mean that it would take me nearly 40 minutes if I drove to work, and when I was forced to take public transport one time it took me nearly an hour door to door. Even this was not the real reason.

Anxiety has plagued me for as long as I can remember. On a bus I feel the eyes of others upon me and struggle to cope with that for more than a few minutes. Late at night on a reasonably empty bus this is not an issue, but as part of a daily commute it feels like I am being strangled. Ironically, I've travelled and coped with overcrowded trains in major cities without a problem. Away from home I feel like a spectator in the audience of someone else's production. Every journey is an adventure. On the buses at home, I am an actor on stage. I am the subject of the audience's attention. I am always one look away from being broken.

Children born in Australia in the 1970's commonly counted down the days to their 16th birthday, when they would rush to get their learners permit. They then hurried to get the independence that comes with their driver's licence. Out of boredom I faced up to the learner's test and narrowly passed. Decades later I still haven't driven a car beyond a learning environment. I end up in a lather of sweat, overwhelmed when I get into the driver's seat. It will never be part of my life. The world needs less cars on the road and my so-called weakness is helping me to do my bit. I find it far easier to explain things that way on the many times I'm asked about this supposed peculiar aspect of my life.

The driveway of my block of units is the first moment of discomfort that I face each day. Usually, I manage to avoid having to make eye contact with any of my neighbours, but sometimes this can't be avoided. It may only be a wave, or a *"Hello Anthony"* from them as I ride past, but even this has me on edge. The moment I see a body appear near the driveway, if I can wait, I do.

As my watch ticks to 8.25, I turn right onto the side street that I follow for 40 metres before the next right turn. I feel a sense of triumph that I've escaped the driveway unnoticed. The cars, other bikes, and pedestrians that I'll pass on my journey are inconsequential. If I don't know them, there is no emotional struggle. Maybe someone I know will see me but barring an unusual scenario arising, I now face twenty-eight minutes without interaction until I arrive at work.

It is rare that I see someone I know on my way into town. The scarcity of this reminds me of how irrelevant I am. From the hundreds of people at my school, to the additional people that have come into my life each year since, the sum total is still just a tiny proportion of the city's population. Even in the suburbs that I've been part of throughout my life, I am anonymous. Most people are. Most people can disappear from the face of the earth, and it would be barely noticed. More than most, it will be the case for me.

It always feels colder when you first start riding. Cutting through the wind on a bike feels significantly colder than walking in the same conditions. I'm not going back on my view of the weather being ideal, but ideal is cool, at least through the first part of the ride. It is very much a standard Adelaide May morning. Anytime people begin to set expectations around averages they usually get disappointed. People often ask me when I travel about what the weather will be like in a particular place. I remind them of the unpredictability of our weather. Adelaide in May might generally be temperate, but it will include unseasonably warm or cold days. The same applies everywhere else. People recommend going certain places at certain times of the year because that is when the weather is ideal. Almost without exception, that is a misnomer. It may more frequently be ideal, but weather is always half-chance. You can prepare all you like for average, but at any time be prepared to add or subtract ten to fifteen degrees from that. Today's forecast is nineteen and whether that is right or wrong there is every chance that by the end of the week we could face a deluge of rain or a spike in temperature to just over thirty. I haven't had the need to check the forecast for the week, but neither would surprise me.

Now that I'm past the neighbours, the vision of Terry and the workplace come back to me. The thoughts of what lay ahead, but more the thoughts of what happened Friday. I know that when I tell Sam the story, Terry will deny everything. When it's his word versus mine, who knows what will be believed. Either way, there won't be action against him without proof. By the end of the day, they'll be certain of the need to do something about him.

CHAPTER 4

FRIDAY MAY 13, 2022

If looks could kill, Terry would be one of the most prolific serial killers in history. He could fire a look across a room that could lay someone out more effectively than the right-hook of a title fighter. His dark features against pale skin added prominence to both. He had a brooding look that screamed out 'stay away,' yet several of the women in the office considered him attractive. With his arrogant persona, I couldn't see how he would appeal to anyone other than himself. The permanent sneer on his face should turn anyone off. True, he may be in decent shape for his age, a perfect contrast to me, but so what? When those dark eyes locked in, he looked ferocious. I guess that works for some people.

The words barely mattered. With just his glare, I knew he was angry, and assumed I was the cause. I tried to think of why. Usually I had an inkling, but this time I was clueless.

'Shut the door,' he said, in order that the tirade to come was at least partly muffled from the rest of the staff on the floor.

'What's up,' I asked while avoiding direct eye contact.

'I heard what you were talking about at lunch.'

As uncomfortable as it was, I now looked directly at him. He had most certainly not heard what I was talking about at lunch, for he wasn't anywhere nearby. At best, he has heard a version of what I said at lunch. Given there was nothing connected to him, I found it highly unlikely that what had offended him had borne any relationship to my conversation.

Like most days, I had eaten lunch with my colleagues Brooke and Ezra. I trusted both of them implicitly and knew they wouldn't have said anything. More significantly, I knew that they dreaded Terry more than I did and would not have done anything to stay in his presence a moment longer than necessary. The only other person in the meal room was Rachel, one of the new staff. I barely knew her, but noticed her sitting on her own in the corner. She had to be his source, but surely she couldn't have heard our conversation.

'Someone has told you what I said, have they? And how certain was this person? How certain are you that they're not looking to score brownie points with you and making up a story for that purpose?'

'They have credibility. You're a proven liar.'

'That is bullshit.' I had lied to him before, albeit on the most trivial of matters. He never let that go. In this case the truth was behind me, and I could prove it.

'Thanks to your ongoing witch hunts, I've started recording every fucking minute that I sit in that meal room with anyone else. I can play back the entire lunchtime and you'll see that you and this whole fucking branch never once came up in conversation. All that will be left is to work out whether your little spies are misinterpreting things, or just making up outright lies.'

'You could've turned that on and off at any moment. It won't prove a thing,' he said.

'You don't care about the truth at all, do you?' I paused for a moment, trying to make sense of this ridiculous discussion. 'It is all just a game to you, isn't it? You are just here to feather your own nest. Push your people up, get rid of those you don't like and try and build your own little power base. Live in a little fantasy world where your life has some sort of relevance.'

'You and I both applied for this job, and they had no hesitation selecting me. You need to remember who has relevance. It ain't you. Jump off the roof and nobody would give a shit.'

I stared back at him with a similar harshness to what he was directing at me. I could believe this was his attitude. I couldn't believe that he was openly saying it. I was just pissed off I wasn't recording this conversation. *Jump off the roof and nobody would give a shit.* He actually said that.

'I'm not listening to anything more,' I said. 'I'm here to work. You play whatever games you want, but I'm not interested.' I stood and walked to the door, and though he told me to wait, I continued on my way.

'You'll be hearing from Sam,' he said from the doorway before slamming his door hard enough to ensure the entire floor was focussed on us.

I got back to my desk and Ezra asked what had happened. I mentioned the line about killing myself.

'You have to report that,' he said.

'What will be achieved?'

'It draws a line in the sand to stop it continuing,'

I saw Terry disappear into Sam's office to report my so-called behavioural issue. I expected to be called in, but all the managers within the branch had a meeting to attend straight afterwards, so I was temporarily spared. Madeleine would be next to hear Terry's version of events at the start of that meeting. She knew him well enough to know that his words were worthless. That said, he was skilled enough in the art of manipulation that he'd cover off every hole in his story. He certainly wouldn't mention that he told me to kill myself.

I spent the next hour and a half clock-watching. If only the managers meeting could extend long enough, I'd be able to bolt out the door before facing Sam today. It wasn't going to mean the issue would be forgotten, but if a weekend passed before the next confrontation, the impact was likely to be lessened.

I got an email from a former colleague who was requesting a reference. Mai had worked in a few different teams within our branch, having me as her team leader on multiple occasions. She was a hard worker, thorough in approach and accurate in all she did. She exceeded performance in every task set for her and was a role model for others to follow. Such performance has its rewards in most workplaces. Not with our management.

'Everyone has to do a stint in the call centre,' Sam said. 'We have to be equitable to all. Equity and diversity underpin this organisation.'

Mai's spoken English was poor. There was no prospect of her being understood on the phones. As hard as she tried, she couldn't meet the performance standards in that role. The team leader had to intervene on most calls. Other operators had to take additional calls. Customers got frustrated and often had to call back. Mai's previous role was taken by an inferior worker, so there was loss in more than one area. Mai was left humiliated by the harassment from Terry, her unit manager. He berated her for performance issues that were completely beyond her control. Eventually, Sam found Mai a role in another department. Our branch lost a quality employee. We lost a key element of our diversity.

I am not sure if the handling of Mai was more comedy or tragedy. She ended up in a better environment which was great, but she was put through disgusting treatment along the way. All of this stemmed from the banner of equity, yet it was the most inequitable treatment I had seen.

Equity and diversity underpin this organisation. Equity isn't about treating everyone the same, it is about treating people in a manner that gives them the same opportunity. By misunderstanding equity, we had lost diversity. After moving on our African trainee, our Aboriginal trainee, we'd now lost a Vietnamese employee who was one of our very best. I looked around the office and saw the diverse group Sam had wanted. Young and white, throughout.

Finishing my reply, I looked up and saw that the management meeting had finished. I had to move fast. Madeleine was the first face I saw as I was packing up to leave. 'What happened with Terry. Sam's furious.' I hadn't really needed the heads-up, certain that she'd have jumped on the side of the argument she heard first.

'He's full of shit. You know that. Surely Sam does too.'

'If someone makes a complaint it has to be investigated.'

'If two people give different versions of a story, why is one version accepted as truth without any reasonable basis.'

'It isn't. That's why it is investigated,' she said.

'Did he mention that he told me to kill myself?'

She looked at me incredulously. I explained that I didn't want to go any further into it at this stage, I just wanted to get out of there. She let me, but just as I started to walk to the door, Sam saw me.

'You're on your way? Can we catch up 9am Monday?'

While it was nice that it was asked, it wasn't really a question. I would be meeting her at 9am Monday. I had nothing to be concerned about, for it was Terry that was in the wrong. That is how it should be, but I knew Sam better than that. Once Sam took a position on any issue, she was too irrational to see another side. Despite the seniority of her position, she had little capacity to evaluate alternatives. Her instincts were generally good, but she was far too reliant on them. Good management was dependent on the ability to see the best course to set in any situation. It was equally reliant on the ability to identify when the wrong course has been taken, and to change accordingly. Sam only had half of these prerequisites covered.

When an issue like the one between Terry and I arose, Sam's ability to manage the situation had me concerned. She knew and disliked us both. She would be happy to be on the opposite side to both of us in most arguments, but when we were already on opposite sides, where would she sit. Knowing her patterns, she was more likely to align with the story she heard first. Would she then even listen to my side of the story.

Terry's words had been so offensive that she may refuse to believe it possible that they were said. The truth wasn't relevant. Sam's instincts were what mattered.

Great. A whole weekend to play through this meeting over and again. My mind was not going to stop just on the meeting with Sam. Everything Terry said would be replaying all weekend. How many times would I hear that one most offensive line run through my head? *Jump off the roof and nobody would give a shit.*

CHAPTER 5

8.25AM

I must focus on the road. There's no traffic that force this on me, but it's the only way to get those two faces out of my mind.

The right from my street is followed by a left shortly after, taking me to the intersection with the main road. As a much busier road, the traffic light cycle can mean there is a long wait here. When my timing is fortunate enough, I can make up a couple of minutes in my schedule here. Today luck isn't with me, but the long queue of cars already waiting for the lights has me suspecting the wait will be short. Almost all of these are in the left lane waiting to go straight, while I sit behind a solitary car in the designated turn right lane.

My insecurities become overwhelming when I feel the eyes of others on me, yet when I delve deeply enough into people watching, I am the spectator and I have control. I may only have 30 seconds stuck on this spot before red turns to green, but I use this time to look at other people starting their days and create my version of what awaits them. Some people are daily fixtures along this route, but at this intersection, it is usually new faces and new stories every day.

The car in front has a golden retriever sitting in the back seat. There is something about his expression as he looks back at me that brings a smile to my face, something that has seemed impossible for a long time. He doesn't focus on me for long before he sticks his head out of the window to see what is happening on that side of the vehicle. The dog seems to enjoy people watching as much as I do. I realise that dog watching is more enjoyable, though maybe less thought provoking than its human equivalent.

A quick glance to my left sees the lengthy line of vehicles that is a cross section of my suburb. The four-wheel drive that has never gone off the streets of our suburbs is first in line with its two children in the back seat on its way to school. Mum in the driver's seat seems like she is counting down the minutes until they're no longer her problem and the freedom she craves awaits. She looks a lot like a neighbour I had growing up, so I christen her Tracey as I wrestle over the plans I imagine for her. Maybe she will be catching up with a group of other mothers to meet at the upmarket shopping centre. They will lie about how wonderful their lives, their husbands and their children all are in order to justify their own existence to themselves. Alternatively, I consider her enthusiasm for the drop off may be motivated by a planned rendezvous with an illicit lover. Is it her husband's friend? A younger man? A woman?

I dare not allow myself to go deeper into these thoughts while waiting at the lights, so I look directly to my left at the next car in line. A Lamborghini Roadster being driven by a man in his early fifties who is intent on believing he is half that age. He craves attention, and although it's the attention of attractive twenty-something women that he mainly seeks, he gets a kick out of any set of eyes that stay on him and his car. I am unwilling to do anything to satisfy his wishes. Someone with the resources to do something for the greater good, but he is so desperate for attention that he blows a quarter of a million dollars on a car. There are many problems with our world. People like him are one of them.

I notice a girl walking on the footpath opposite the flow of traffic on the road. If not for the school uniform she was wearing, I'd have thought she was in her twenties, as she looks older and more mature than some of the women in our office. Despite her age, she is close enough to be Mr. Lamborghini's target market. I like her, if for no other reason than her eyes remaining straight ahead, and not on the show pony. He even revved the engine as she passed to ensure attention, but she kept her view on the footpath. I think she looks like a Sophie, so she will stay in my memory under that name. She's looked up at someone walking on the other side of the road. She isn't closed off to the world, just those unworthy of her attention. People should be more like Sophie.

Thankfully, my mind is distracted as I look back in front and see the dogs tail wagging. The lights have turned red on the main road and in turn are now green for us. Enthusiastic mum takes off followed by Mr. Lamborghini. The car in front of me has rolled into the intersection, waiting there for the vehicles coming the other way to pass before she can complete her turn. I've rolled forward with her and sit 30 centimetres behind the back of her car, a point from which I won't be moving until the lights change again and the oncoming traffic is forced to stop, allowing us to complete our turns.

I keep an eye on the inside lane and the array of vehicles passing. One other bike passed through on the bicycle lane, along with a tradesman in a van on the way to his next job. There were men headed to office jobs, more parents dropping kids at schools and the odd person for whom I had insufficient time to contemplate. I glance back as the amber light comes on, and briefly I divert at least some level of attention away from the golden retriever. I keep my safe distance and focus on the car. She turns and I follow.

CHAPTER 6

SATURDAY SEPTEMBER 20, 1980

She turns and I follow. It hasn't come quickly or easily, but my mother is patient. She is teaching me to ride a bicycle and has told me that today she would take the training wheels off. I don't think she will. She has threatened it before and not done it. When she does, I will give up and go inside.

I follow Mum down the driveway and into the garage, around the post and back to the top of the driveway. We've been doing this every day since I got the bike. It's fun. I like riding a bike, but I only like doing it because I can do it my way, with the training wheels keeping me safe, and nobody seeing me if something goes wrong.

Everyone says I'm a scaredy-cat. I don't like to try anything new they say. I guess I do tend to run away when things don't work out right. Mum always talks about how I didn't learn to walk until very late. I think I tried when nobody was looking, failed and then gave up on ever doing it. I still do things like that. I don't want anyone to see me fail in anything, so I only try when nobody will see.

When I was three, our family went on a cruise. I don't really remember much about it, but I got very sick. When we arrived in Fiji, I was taken straight to hospital and that's where I stayed for the whole time we were there. When the ship was due to leave and head back to Australia, I was allowed out of hospital. I still needed to be given a lot of medication. When the doctor on the ship had to give me an injection, I got scared. I'd had them before, and they hurt. I jumped up, spun around and bolted, but ran straight into a wall, knocking myself out. Now I'm even more scared of injections.

Ever since we got back from Fiji, I have kept getting sick. I have spent so much time in hospital ever since, but Mum says I was never sick before we went away. Maybe things work in patterns, so that once one bad thing happens, the next just follows. Dad says that isn't true and it only seems like bad things happen when you start expecting it.

'Be positive, and good things will happen. Believe that you can ride the bike and you will be able to do it,' he said before he went to work this morning.

I don't like our house. I miss our old house, but we can't go back. We lived in the hills, but on Ash Wednesday there was a big fire. Our house burned down. Mum and Dad said that our dog Cindy and our cat Blackie both ran away.

'They didn't run away, they got burnt to death,' my brother Tom said.

'Don't say that. You'll cause more problems and you have no idea whether it is true,' Mum said directly to him.

'Yeah, right, they ran away and they're alright' Tom said to Vanessa and me. I felt relieved but Vanessa didn't seem to believe him.

There are sounds, sights and smells that mean I will always remember that day. The sirens of fire brigades. The smell of smoke. The bright orange flames. We weren't home, but the whole sky glowed and even from Mum and Dad's shop in town, we could see it. We didn't know that it had reached our house, but by the time Dad rushed towards home to save what he could, it was too late.

Now we live in a house near the schools that Tom and Vanessa go to. It is also not far from Mum and Dad's shop. They say we won't be here for too long, but we are not going back to the hills. They are scared that there will be more fires. Even though I liked it there, I don't want to ever have that sort of fear again.

After lunch, the training wheels had been taken off. Dad, Tom and Vanessa were all out, so it was just Mum and me at home. If it was only Mum who saw me fail, it wouldn't be so bad, right? She stood in front of the bike, holding onto the handlebars. She had me on the bike, my bottom on the seat and my feet on the ground. She then moved behind the bike and showed me how to scoot. I kept my right foot on the right pedal and pushed off with my left foot. Before I started, I had both hands over the brakes and I put them on again to stop. Mum got me to do this several times. No pedalling, but I kept getting better and better with my balance.

Next, she held the seat from behind me as I pedalled.

I can do it! At least with Mum holding me. Hang on, she isn't holding me. So, I'm actually doing it all on my own. Well, I had been doing it all on my own. Almost as soon as I knew it was all me, I lost my balance and fell. It didn't hurt so badly, but I was crying as though it was the worst pain ever.

'You let go,' I yelled through my tears. If there was one part of me truly wounded, it was my pride. Failure hurts me more than anything.

'It's alright. Everyone falls when they are learning. You're not badly hurt.'

'Yes I am.' I was generally a quiet child, but once I got loud, I got very loud.

'Take a few minutes and we'll try again,' she said.

'No. I will not,' I screamed. I picked the bike up, only so that I could throw it back to the ground in anger. 'I'm never riding a bike again.'

CHAPTER 7

8.26AM

Clearly, I did. A few years later I had made friends with people who rode bikes all the time so I would have been a social pariah had I not been able to do so. When I moved to a school further from home, cycling wasn't an option, and I virtually stopped using my bike for a couple of years. Again, it was friends who cycled that got me back into it again in my mid-teens. Ever since that time, I've never gone more than a few days off a bike.

I pretty much cycle everywhere, but a lot of noise seems to pass through my head during each journey. I used to sing songs inside my head to pass the time. On remote enough roads I might start singing out loud. Particularly when pushing up hills, it always seemed easier to avoid thinking of the challenge of the road by focusing my mind on something else. I suppose I am still doing that now, but rather than having songs in my head, it is little bits of everything. Often it has me thinking of things I don't want in my head, and it is completely beyond my control. The more I try to avoid a particular thought the more it will circle continuously. More than anything this is the reason I people-watch, trying to create stories for their lives. If I am focused enough on other people, I can avoid myself. Unfortunately, the brain is sufficiently powerful to turn a fantasy-inspired stranger into someone with a connection to some part of my life. Sometimes even without a connection I still end up back at the same uncomfortable points.

Out of nowhere, Olivia pops into my head. Not quite nowhere, for she's never far away. Whenever I hear someone say that time heals all wounds, I know they are wrong. Some wounds can never heal. Olivia will always be proof of that.

Without closure, is it possible to move forward? The term closure isn't necessarily straight forward. There are scenarios where genuine closure can be virtually impossible. Even then, there is always some scope with which a line can be drawn under an event to aid the process of moving on. Maybe I have just failed in my attempts to draw this line. Cleo was the source of great pain and regret for me, but I moved on. Other examples show where I have dismally failed. The wounds from Olivia are as raw as they were at the time. Other wounds are far older and still have their grip on me. Don't point me to counselling as I've been there, felt like I've progressed, only to find myself a bad day away from sinking further than ever before.

I hate my job. Every day I feel the life get sucked further out of me as I perform a range of mindless tasks that a trained monkey could do. I had often said that if I dropped dead in the office, the only sadness that would be felt would be because of the paperwork they needed to complete. A few days later the memories of me would begin to fade and before too long nobody would remember me or anything I had ever done. That was refuted by the people that I'd built good relationships with, but when I stressed that I was referring to the management of the branch, they understood and agreed.

I don't have a need to be remembered, but it's hard to feel good about spending half my waking hours in a workplace wasting time. Where I am there is nothing to achieve. I am nothing more than a tiny insignificant cog in the massive piece of machinery that is the government sector. Forgettable, replaceable, and insignificant.

The route I take to work never varies, even though on the ride home I alternate between several different pathways. Three years ago, I attended a Christmas breakfast function for all the managers when the topic of riding to work came up. Our IT manager Richard was encouraging Patrick to join us as bicycle commuters.

'Before too long you find the best route' he said

'I did and I married her, but what's that got to do with cycling to work,' he said. Patrick could have been a professional footballer in his younger years but I suspect he lacked the necessary work ethic. He learned the lessons from that, and his approach in the workplace now is the epitome of professionalism. There may be little intrusions of political incorrectness in moments like these, yet they seem to endear him to the right people. Sometimes the difference between personality aiding or hindering your career in our branch is the finest of lines.

We have eighty people in our office, and in the years I have been there, I suspect I've worked with a couple of hundred more. Most of these people have enriched my life and have been great to work with. I have different but unique friendships that I value with a range of people. While work is what links us all, talking sport with Patrick, having a laugh with Ezra, or discussing world affairs with Madeleine, all help me get through the day, which makes me the most productive I can be. Uniting with people and establishing meaningful relationships adds satisfaction and reason to the day. It is only natural we achieve more in these circumstances, though Sam and Terry can't see this. They work that way themselves, but think such things shouldn't apply to lower ranking staff.

When I was acting in the section manager role, I sat alongside Madeleine, helping develop the next generation of leaders within the branch. Our management team had differences, but these connected in such a way to optimise results. Our varied approaches and beliefs were underpinned by respect between all of us. Disagreements were respectful. Unity was the goal and generally achieved. Whenever anyone had to give ground, they did so willingly with consensus being the target we always strived to meet.

Terry provided a vastly different dynamic. Whatever his politics, his managerial approach seemed more suited to a chain gang than an office. Shoot first, ask questions later. No. Don't ask questions at all. There was an irrational view to his approach with people. He fired temporary staff if they were absent more than once, despite us not paying for their absences.

'I'm not keeping someone here who has that sort of attitude,' he said, referring to Russell. Russell was a contractor who'd been with us for a month before three days of sick leave. Had he been at work, coughing, spluttering, and probably infecting others we'd have been far more out of pocket.

Instead, a good worker was gone without replacement. In a couple of weeks someone new would arrive, waste more of our staff's time training them with a fair likelihood of survival for no longer than Russell. At a whim, Terry's ire would see them gone too. In the meantime, backlogs extended through being short staffed. It was all idealistically sound. He set ambitious standards and didn't suffer fools. In a perfect world, it would be an ideal strategy. Our workplace was far from ideal, and provisions had to be made for this.

Once he'd returned to the branch and I returned to my old role, I had little to do with Sam and Madeleine. I knew how the dynamic worked. Rather than being in the same meetings discussing staff across the branch, I was now one of the people being talked about. With Terry being my immediate manager, whatever was being said about me, was being done so through a narrow view. Madeleine, my long-term ally, wasn't in the position to defend me. She would hear but get little opportunity to speak. I'd been there, so I knew how it worked.

The damage that was being done across the branch was noticeable to everyone. Terry's approach made enemies, not just among staff on the floor, but with management too. He'd become the bane of Sam's existence, but there was little within her scope to change things. She was doing what she could to find external opportunities for him, but he didn't seem that interested. He wanted to move up, not out and across again.

I need to get away from thinking about work on the ride. Day by day my whole ride to work was being spent replaying conversations I'd had with Terry and modifying them to the things I wish I had said. Terry became a huge factor in my deteriorating sleep habits and worsening health. After a few months, Sam realised that it was futile trying to get us to work together effectively, so I was allocated to a role under Madeleine. The work was almost the same but in not reporting to Terry, my levels of stress diminished greatly. Ironically once I was not reporting to him, our relationship became much better. Moments like Friday proved that there was still an undercurrent lurking.

Time is such a strange concept. They say it flies when you're having fun, but the figure of speech only tells part of the story. When work is slow, an hour in the office feels like a day. When we're flat out, it certainly can't be confused with being fun, but the time does go fast. Busy, be it fun or otherwise, and you don't have time to watch the clock. It is how much you think about the passing time that defines how fast it goes. Five minutes waiting for a bus has always felt like an eternity. Five minutes on my ride to work is the blink of an eye.

Long time frames work differently. Weeks, months and years require a different reflection. People all seem to agree that every year goes by quicker. It's more than a feeling. It's impossible not to perceive it that way. Our concept of time comes from our experience of it. At the age of five, our eyes see a year as 20% of a lifetime. At fifty, the same year is 2% of a lifetime. This is how we all see time, and it is why 2021 was ten times quicker than 1981 was for me. When the school holidays were four weeks away, it felt so far out of reach as to be barely imaginable. Now, four weeks away from annual leave and it feels like the home stretch. Time itself doesn't accelerate, but we cannot see or touch time, merely perceive it. Through our perceptions, it constantly accelerates.

Our workplace has people under twenty and others over sixty. Do they experience this different perception? Massively. The twenty-year-olds all seem to walk in faster and more enthusiastically each morning, only to struggle with the first moment when things settle and they take their first look at the clock. The older workers trudge in, dreading what lies ahead, only to need a reminder that it's break time, so quickly that it has arrived. Being half-way between, I trudge like the oldies and clock-watch like the youth. To be fair, that has less to do with my perception of time, and more my desire to be anywhere else.

Terry has a similar desire, though I'm sure our happy places couldn't be more different. When I met him, he presented such a strong persona that I instantaneously formed a clear-cut view of him. As I got to know him this changed dramatically. I could see how much the person within differed from the image he presented. He wasn't powerful, he was insecure. He'd scream loud so that nobody was exposed to the weakness that shone through in the silence. He made sure he got so many words out that nobody had a chance to focus on how meaningless most of his words were. I have a bitter working relationship with him, far more so than I have ever had with a colleague, yet it doesn't necessarily mean I dislike him more than all others. Who is the real Terry? I feel like most of the problems come when he is being least true to the person within and masks up to deliver the role of 'Manager Terry.' He thinks bravado earns credibility. Maybe this is closer to who he really is? Have I been sucked in at other times by the Terry who seems more genuine, more vulnerable, and more intelligent? Maybe this is the fake version?

Every day I make up scenarios about strangers based on an initial view. How can I possibly expect these to be accurate? Maybe the woman I was next to at the lights has no unethical plans for her day. Maybe Sophie would have fawned over Mr. Lamborghini but was just so deep in her own mind she didn't notice him. Any judgement comes from our own experiences and biases. We always guess. Sometimes we are right. People watchers will look at me and think a variety of things most of which will be a long way from the truth. I think people could look at me and think *that guy looks like he has completely lost the will to live.* Is that what anyone else sees?

I have a love-hate relationship with life, and I have a love-hate relationship with this commute. On a good day I arrive at work in the best possible state following the relaxation, fresh air, and gentle exercise that the short ride provides me. Other days, I am so emotionally exhausted from where my mind has gone that I'm ready to go home before the day begins.

Even though I ride slowly, I'm rarely passed by bikes on this road. Few cyclists use it as it's not bike friendly. A narrow two-lane road with no bicycle lane leaves you feeling vulnerable. During peak hour there is no decent traffic flow. Most vehicles stick to the middle of their lanes allowing me to ride through on the left, enabling me to move swifter than the cars. Unfortunately, some drivers have no idea of the width of their vehicles, and one such car is virtually in the gutter waiting for the next opportunity to move a car length. As a result, I am obstructed and must carefully move between him and the car behind to get into the centre of the two lanes. From there I get around Gutterman and return to my spot on the left-hand side of the road.

In the same way as I did at the lights, I end up noticing things or people that occupy my mind. Often my mind runs into complete tangents with these people, other times it might be more relevant thought. Something can trigger a reminder of past events and a complete episode of my life plays out in my mind in the space of a few moments. I've lived long enough to have sufficient good and bad memories that this can be either a wonderful or terrible thing. It generally beats the hell out of just looking at the road ahead, though of course there are times when I wish my mind would go quiet.

I notice Robin Williams walking along the other side of the road. Not the comedian of course, but a lookalike. Well to be honest he doesn't look like him at all, but a couple of years ago I noticed him and dubbed him Robin Williams. He walks along the footpath each morning and afternoon with something like a school bag on his shoulder. He is way too old to be at school. I have no idea where he goes, but he is like clockwork. About 8.35 he hits Glen Osmond Road where he waits for a bus heading towards the hills. After seeing him and his pattern at least a hundred times I saw him up close and was disappointed at how little resemblance there was to the man I named him after. It doesn't matter, he is only Robin Williams in the conversations in my head. I don't need to justify that.

I don't give names to everyone I pass, just those that stand out. The people I see often stand out to me. Some of them look like someone I know and get their name that way. Sometimes, like Robin Williams, they get their name from someone famous or fictional character. Often on the same stretch of road I see Keith Flint, a man who bares absolutely no resemblance to the singer from the Prodigy. He just stood out to me and needed a name, but I was listening to a Prodigy song at the time and named him accordingly. It was just timing, but the name stuck. There are two guys I've dubbed the two Dan's, after rugby player Dan Vickerman. They look alike, so I assumed they were brothers, but they carry themselves more like a couple. I've never worked that out, but 'Two-Dan's' are now part of my day. Between all of these "friends" I feel like my lonely ride to work also serves as my major daily social interaction. Within the confines of my lonely life, my imaginary friendships with Keith, Robin, Two Dan's and others are as good as I have.

It's very unusual so early, but a familiar couple has turned the corner. I don't have a name for these two, possibly because I don't enjoy thinking about them. They are a young couple, with a baby just a few months old. Since Olivia, babies have always been a cause of discomfort, but in this instance my issue is the parents. The sunken eyes, the gaunt faces, the scratched, acne-ridden skin, and the dental disaster combined to scream out meth-heads. What hope does this child have? His parents are little more than kids themselves and they're junkies. They live in a block of low-cost housing that seems full of the same type, so they're not likely to ever escape it. Through work, I've seen far too many examples of people living these lifestyles and it always ends up ugly. When it's just themselves paying the price, I couldn't really care. When a child has no escape, it's a tragedy waiting to happen.

I know enough about tragedies. Even if it is only from a short-lived stage of life in a very different time, I ended up getting to know enough about meth too.

CHAPTER 8

SATURDAY SEPTEMBER 9, 2003

'Maybe you need something different. Have something that's gonna be more effective at picking you up than just another drink. Live up to your name Speedy,' Dylan said.

I'd worked with Dylan for about a year. We got along well enough in the office, and occasionally went for a quick drink after work, but our socialising rarely extended beyond that. I got the impression that he was a little too wild for me. He was a couple of years younger than me, but he looked like a generation below. His clothes, his hair, his attitude. I may have a childlike lack of responsibility, but that combines with several attributes more in keeping with an old-man's approach to life. Dylan was the wild and untamed young adult who played by his own rules. The two-year age gap seemed to massively understate the difference between us.

He never specified what he took. Maybe he had, but by using his standard street slang, I never understood. I did know that his weekends involved far more than drinking. With us both at a party held by a former colleague, I was getting the opportunity to see a little more of what he was like.

'You've never tried speed, Bourdain?'

'A long time ago,' I said, but not so sure about the accuracy of the statement. In the final year of school, I was told that some dope I was smoking had been laced with speed, but I didn't notice anything. Either the impact was far less significant than had been suggested, or more likely I'd been duped.

At over thirty, I should be well past the point of susceptibility to peer pressure, but when he persisted after my initial rejection, I quickly relented. While he snorted a line, I just mixed mine in my drink. The effect supposedly is slower acting, but it still produced the effect Dylan had promised. I was energised. It didn't seem to be an artificial high, just a level of enthusiasm for the party that was uncharacteristic of me. For the first time in my life, I was out on the dancefloor. I had the necessary feeling of liberation to hit on whoever I wanted, and although things didn't quite go my way in that respect, it didn't diminish the mildly euphoric feeling that had built within me.

After the party, Dylan and I headed into town and went to a few clubs in and around Hindley Street. Normally my nights are winding down soon after midnight, but tonight I was going strong until sunrise, oblivious to the movement of time. I never took anything more than the first dose that Dylan had given me. I hadn't felt anything too overwhelming, yet I just wasn't winding down.

We'd been in a bar that closed at sunrise. I still felt like it was mid-evening. The fast-food outlets were the only places open, now serving breakfast. I didn't feel like food. I didn't know what I felt like, but it wasn't like any other Sunday morning.

'The casino is still open,' Dylan said.

'Let's do it.'

Casinos and a heightened sense of confidence are not an ideal combination. Initially we grabbed drinks but before too long we were lured into the table games. I blew $500 without realising what I was doing. Dylan, who was down $15 found it amusing.

'Get fucked,' I said a little too loudly.

I didn't survive in there for long. Security were on me in moments. I won't be going back there anytime soon, but that suits me.

I won't be touching anything else that's offered to me like that either.

*

I don't know how I feel today. I haven't slept for 36 hours but don't feel any form of tiredness. I don't feel hungover in the traditional sense but there is something that doesn't feel right. I guess coming down from that kind of high is bound to have an impact, but it's not in the overpowering way I thought it would be.

I'm not an idiot. I know the dangers and I don't want to let myself fall into the trap of a regular habit. Anything on the odd occasion can't be too much of an issue. The only problems came right at the end of the night when I shouldn't have still been out. I should have found someone to take home and been making better use of my stamina. That was the mistake, not the meth.

I think.

*

It's not a problem. In the six weeks since I first tried meth with Dylan, I have used it increasingly regularly, but it's only just to add a little to nights. During the week it gives me a bit more ability to go out and enjoy a night and then still be alright for work the next morning. I don't need it, but it just adds a little something.

Sex is amazing when high. I've seen this girl named Greta a couple of times. She's wild. I don't think I could find a single point of interest in her when straight, but once we're high, we don't leave the bedroom. Our one point of compatibility.

It does kind of suck being at work coming down, but I can't get away with pulling sickies. I've got no leave left, so I must keep turning up. After the nights I've been having, it is the last place I want to be, so I've started taking a little something to get me through the day. It might keep me awake, but it makes every element of my day there so much more drawn out. It feels like an afternoon takes about three weeks. I know people are noticing stuff here. I'm not sure if they know what it is, but they know somethings different. Maybe Dylan has talked. He started all this, but he's been distant of late. He did chat to me last week and advised me to cut back a bit. What the fuck? Ah, maybe he is right.

*

I haven't touched meth for a month now. I am adamant I never will again. Whether I liked to admit it or not, I didn't like the person I was becoming. As far as I could see, not too many other people did either.

Within a month, I lost my job, I moved in with Greta, I broke up with Greta, I stopped sleeping properly, even when not using, I was having regular nausea and had two bad panic attacks. I don't know how much any of it had to do with the meth, but the more I consumed, the more issues I had.

I haven't had a good day since I quit, but to be honest, I didn't have too many good days in the last few months I was using. The major difference is that now I give a shit about it.

I've moved into Dad's house. That is a challenge to say the least, though I'm sure it is just as much that way for him as me. I have got a job, albeit only a couple of shifts a week. At least there are a few dollars coming in and I'm getting structure back into my life. I'm not sleeping properly yet, but I'm improving. I'm eating better. I'm drinking no more than a few beers a week. I'm not touching anything more.

Momentum shapes life. I wouldn't have lost my job if not for the meth. I wouldn't have had the meth if not for Dylan. I wouldn't have met Dylan if I'd got a suitable job. I would have got a suitable job if I hadn't have dropped out of school. Where does the line get drawn? In the impressionable years of my youth, I avoided the temptation of drugs. At a time when my vulnerability should have long passed, I took for granted my ability to retain control. I set a downward trajectory, and piece by piece everything came crashing down.

I don't have a lot of self-respect, but there are some things I can see clearly. I didn't want to be me, but I sure as hell do not want to be the person I was becoming. Most people don't turn that around. I haven't got much, but that is one thing I woke up proud of this morning.

CHAPTER 9

8.27am

As I get close to bus stop 7, I see four people waiting. This is usually a quiet stop, so there mustn't have been a bus for some time. That suits me, as it means I'm not going to have a bus blocking me up ahead. Buses can be a significant obstacle along this road. Whereas I have space to the left of all other traffic, buses leave minimal room in the stop-start nature of peak hour. They are frequently enough back to the curb making their stops and squeezing out the few cyclists that use this road. Thursday mornings I can face the same obstacle from the rubbish collection truck, but usually my timing is good enough to avoid that.

I look at the four people. Three of them are familiar to me, but only through this daily game of people watching. First is Virginia Woolf. While others tend to stand back from the road some distance, Virginia is close enough that I can reach out and high-five her. Naturally I don't, but it just adds to the character in my mind. It's so Virginia. Twice I have run into her when I have been with people, and when mentioning the Virginia name, they have given me quizzical looks. I realised in those times that the resemblance is minimal. To be honest, it is downright non-existent, but after years of passing her at this bus stop day after day, there is no chance of me changing the identity in my mind now. When we are dealing with people's existence in my mind there is no need for accuracy and authenticity. Like Robin and Keith, Virginia made sense initially which is all that matters.

Several metres further back from the road is Vincent. The red hair and beard gave him a real Van Gogh look. Well, not really. but a redhead with a beard, it makes sense to go to Vincent. It did occur to me that I never usually saw him here unless I was considerably earlier than today. I wasn't sure whether this was an indication of how late the buses were running or if there was some other issue going on in Vincent's life. I tended to over-analyse these people's lives like that. He had a look of great impatience on his face, so he was evidently far more concerned with the lateness of the buses than the others at the stop. Through this I again felt the pleasure of the far more controllable schedule I had with cycling as my mode of transport.

I would have devoted more thought to Vincent if it wasn't for noticing Ellie at the bus stop. It had been a couple of weeks since I had seen Ellie, so named for her resemblance to the snowboarder Ellie Soutter. I'd read an article on her just after seeing my Ellie, and at first thought it had to be her. Obviously it wasn't, but this girl would always be Ellie to me. It was nice to know that everything was alright after not seeing her recently. I shouldn't be emotionally attached to some-one with whom my only contact was quickly cycling past a couple of times a week, yet somehow these people had a hold on me. I tend to give quite a bit of a background to explain these people. At bus stop 7, Ellie was always a more appealing distraction than what Vincent or Virginia would ever be.

I often drifted into imaginary conversations with Ellie. She would call me Ant rather than Anthony just as Tara always did. Tara went out with me briefly in my mid-teens. There were so many forgettable things about Tara, yet for some reason I'd always felt besotted by her, and the memories never faded. The only other times in life that anyone had called me Ant, I was reminded of her. The excitement a teenage boy feels with his first sexual experiences with a young girl never get surpassed and it is amazing how the name Ant had become a trigger word to relive those feelings, even if it wasn't meant that way by the others who used it.

Ellie wouldn't be half my age, so it isn't appropriate for me to be focusing too much on her. I rarely get along too well with millennials, so although she catches my eye, I wouldn't want that ruined by actually getting to know her. As attractive as Ellie is, I can't go beyond seeing a girl like that, smiling and moving on. It seems strange but sometimes we can enjoy a fantasy even though we'd hate the reality. I guess when we fantasise, it works on the same principles that applies when naming strangers on the street. We distort accuracy for convenience. Thinking of Ellie, I'm not a middle-aged man thinking about a woman in her early twenties. In that moment, I am teenaged Ant once again, and Ellie is cast in the role of Tara, but embellished to remove the bad ending.

The fourth person at the stop was a boy in a private school uniform, probably about fifteen. Maybe this kid had a free period to start the day, or maybe he was awaiting a lift from a passing car belonging to a friend. There could be many things that don't indicate the same sort of misbehaviour that defined my youth, but that still was the natural way my mind ventured.

So often I would head to town from the bus stop at this time of the morning instead of catching the school bus headed in the opposite direction. Public transport to school was limited, so I always had the excuse that if I did miss the bus, I couldn't be there before 10am. I used this to the absolute limit. Ironically, most times that I *missed the bus* were on the days when I left home earliest, eager for adventure. It was usually innocent enough, either heading to a games arcade to play the latest video games for an hour or so. Other times it was just hanging out with my mate Griffin, wandering through the main streets in the city. Once we got a little heat from school we would turn up on time for a while until it seemed like the focus had shifted to someone or something else.

CHAPTER 10

THURSDAY JULY 18, 1991

Daniel was adamant they would serve him.

'There are not too many advantages to being a little person, but at least I get this. Everyone's too bloody afraid of appearing insensitive that they never ask me for ID anywhere. As long as I take the blazer and school tie off, there is no way they'll knock me back.'

Griffin, Sean, Daniel and I got off the bus at the stop near the park. We'd pooled our money, and Daniel was now heading over the road to the bottle shop. The rest of us made our way towards the park, stopping at a vantage point where we could see Daniel. If he wasn't served, there was no plan B. We'd all be home close to the normal time for a school day. When he came out of the bottle shop, our vantage point proved futile. If he had been served, the bottles were in his bag. We still wouldn't know the result until he was back across the road.

We watched the strange but familiar walking action getting closer. He looked up, and the smile said more than words.

'Time for a drink, gentlemen.'

We walked along the pathway, swilling vodka and bourbon respectively, straight from the bottles. Although just set back from the busy road, the park was completely obscured from passers-by. Despite it being a nice day, there wasn't anyone else in the section of the park we were moving into. We kept sharing the bottles around, running around the park and playing on the playground equipment. All of that was helping the booze go straight to our heads and our stomachs. I was already feeling messy, not long after we'd started.

We were so drunk. We were running around the park, out of control. Griffin and I were still in full uniform. It was an accident waiting to happen, with someone surely likely to see us and reporting us to the school. It seemed even more likely when it turned out a former teacher from the school was in the park. But Mr. Russo wasn't going to say a word. Not when we had just seen his hand up the skirt of a girl in school uniform. Drunk as we were, we were more than willing to engage him in conversation.

'Hey, Mr. Russo,' Daniel slurred 'we miss ya man.'

He was panicked at being sprung, but also could see what state we were in. He seemed to think he had that as leverage. While his interaction with a schoolgirl would have much graver consequences than us drinking in school uniform, he knew that the likelihood of us causing him trouble was minimal. He was no longer at our school and from my perspective he hadn't been a particularly menacing figure when there anyway. Everyone was going to be better off walking away and forgetting what they'd seen. He made the excuse that the girl was his cousin. He was just tutoring her. They thought the pleasant outdoor environment would help but they now realised concentration might be easier at home. Clearly, he didn't know how long we'd been watching. Anything he was teaching her was not from any school syllabus.

We laughed that of all the places we'd found for our Thursday night drinks we'd picked the place that our perverted former teacher had already found for his misbehiviour.

'Proves the point that it's a discreet location, right,' Griffin said.

While I laughed, I also felt a little sick as I thought about the idea of a teacher abusing his position like that. I felt conflicted, but I knew for our sakes I'd have to stay quiet. The girl wasn't a student of his and she was a very willing partner. It didn't make it right, but this was a very different case to the likes of the real pervert teachers. The very fact that he was displaying this in public indicated that there was nothing that would appear wrong to the average observer. Russo was probably in his mid-twenties, but he looked barely out of his teens. The girl could have passed for only a couple of years younger than him, whatever the truth happened to be.

After Mr. Russo had gone and we finished the last of our drinks, we decided to head into town. Before we got to the bus stop, two old ladies were walking towards the park. For the rest of us, this was a moment of being quiet, discreet and respectful, but none of these were Daniel's style. He dropped his pants and flashed them.

'Shit man, what are you doing,' I yelled at him, while Griffin and Sean laughed. 'They're bound to ring the school. We're fucked now.'

Struggling to speak or stand properly, Daniel said not to worry.

'They're not gonna ring the school, just like the bottle shop guy wasn't gonna ask me for ID. Same thing.'

We had to walk about a hundred metres down the main road to get to the bus stop. Griffin and Sean were making their way, while I was walking to the edge of the road to look out for buses.

'Guys. Hey guys. There's a bus coming,' I yelled with urgency more like someone seeing a UFO than a bus.

Griffin pointed out that I was the one who was furthest behind, so it was me, not them, who had to get moving. It had become too much for Daniel, who proceeded to lay down on the footpath. I yelled at him to get up, but he didn't, so I kept moving toward the bus stop. Once he saw we weren't waiting, he knew he had no choice, so he got up and moved as quickly as he could to catch up.

I don't know how we didn't get kicked off, but at least it was only ten minutes until we arrived in town. We walked towards Rundle Mall, but Daniel hit the deck again, laying down in the middle of the footpath. Sean started kicking him. It looked like they were severe kicks, but he was in control enough that the foot was going under Daniel's stomach and not making contact.

'My goodness, what are you doing,' a woman cried out running towards us in protection of Daniel.

'Don't worry, we're friends. He loves a good kicking. He's training to be a football,' Sean said. With that, Daniel burst out laughing and the woman shook her head and walked off. Sean left us at that point. He hadn't really got into the spirit of the day or the spirits in the bottle, but his presence may have helped. Everyone would know that a report of a little person and two friends would mean Daniel, Griffin, and me. Three friends and the school won't know who the other person was. Can they act on three people when they know four were equally guilty?

I started singing. Not so much singing as screaming out songs full of obscenities. If Daniel flashing the old women hadn't done it, I was guaranteed to have the school called. Drunk beyond belief, screaming out expletives while dressed in a private school uniform, in the main street of the city. The chances of us getting expelled were growing by the minute.

'Let's go get something to eat,' I said, the sight of the golden arches calling me.

Griffin laughed. 'You won't make it up the stairs. Let's go to Max's instead.'

He was right. It took Daniel and I long enough to get to the Gallerie Arcade without facing stairs. There were a different kind of stares we were facing now. Three exceptionally drunk kids in school uniform had everyone staring. Daniel was used this, but the reason behind it was different now. His reaction wasn't.

'Fuck off,' he said to anyone who stared too long.

We made it to a table inside of Max's, and Griffin went up to buy a few cups of chips as he was the closest to sober out of us. 'What are you looking at,' Daniel said to a kid turning around and staring at us. The kid's father wasn't taking any more of that.

'You are going to turn around, you are going to shut up, and I am not going to hear another word from any of you. If I'm wrong, you're gonna be sorrier than you can imagine. Understand?'

We all nodded. I could tell Daniel was trying to think of a smart-arsed response, but thinking wasn't something any of us were capable of at this stage.

The major crisis came when we realised how few cigarettes we had left. We got going, and in the comparative freedom of the mall, I got back into my previous concert mode, entertaining the people of Adelaide.

"MY ONLY FRIEND, THE END"

'If I had any money left,' Daniel said, 'I would um. Shit, I'm gonna throw up. Nah, it's passed. Man, I'm going to Mum's office, I'll get a lift.'

As we were saying our goodbyes, a middle-aged woman came up to us and said she was going to ring our school to put in a complaint as she'd seen our disgusting behaviour.

'My son went to your school, so I know who to speak to.'

'Yeah, sure,' Daniel said, 'Why don't you just fuck off now and make the call.'

She gave a look of horror then turned and marched off. Daniel still maintained that nothing would happen. Any complaint would only be able to identify us through his disability. The school would never act when that was the means of identification.

Daniel walked down the mall while Griffin and I headed in the opposite direction. At the fountain, we turned and went our separate ways.

'Seeya Griff,' I yelled from about ten metres away.

He turned and waved. I let him go another twenty metres and yelled the same thing again. Again, he turned and waved. I kept this going, getting louder the further he got, still managing to get his attention when he was up at the next set of lights.

'SEEYA GRIFF.'

Shit my throat was sore. Shit my head was sore.

Then I had to face the challenge of getting on a bus and not throwing up before I got home.

*

Would you believe it? Daniel isn't at school today. Griffin isn't at school today. Sean isn't at school today. I am at school today, and I feel so many more levels of shithouse than I can express.

I threw up on the bus last night as we turned into East Terrace. I was so embarrassed, I didn't know what to do, so I rang the bell and got off. I am never catching the 6.04pm bus again. I threw up a few more times in the parklands and then started walking home. Eventually I sat down near the school on Dequetteville Terrace and threw up again. Some guy came up asking me if my parents had forgotten me. I don't know if he was a sicko or if he thought I was from that school, and just waiting for my after-school pick-up. Drunk and not thinking, I gave him my phone number and he said he'd ring Dad.

Obviously, a minute later I realised I'd given some stranger my name and number, so I ran and got on another bus. This time no more vomiting, and as I got off the bus near home, I saw dad's car coming down the street. I ran onto the road and yelled to him. He stopped and picked me up there.

'Drunk or drugs,' he asked?

'Drunk,' I sheepishly said.

Nothing else was said all night, but he made sure I was woken early by being as loud as he could be. There was no relief for my self-imposed sickness. As it turns out, I was the only one who had to face it. Those other buggers are probably still asleep.

All day I've had dirty looks from staff. I'm sure they did get phone calls. I'm sure they're almost certain who it was. The absences tell a story, and the nightmare I look like tells it even clearer. At the beginning of lunch, I got all the necessary proof when the Year 11 form master walked up to me.

'Where do you think Rudolphs and Tudhope are today, Mr Speed?' I felt certain he was speaking as loud as possible to try and ensure that my head copped as much punishment as possible.

'I don't know sir.'

'Really. You don't look the best young man. What a coincidence that those two are both off sick and you look like you should be too. I can't imagine how that could have happened.' His manner had seemed almost friendly when he came over, but his eyes now narrowed and his look turned dark and angry. He then turned and walked away. He knew, but more to the point, I now know that he can't do a thing about it.

Next question is when are we going to do it again?

CHAPTER 11

8.28am

'Shiiiiit.'

Every now and then the monotony of the daily ride into work would be broken in a less than ideal way. With so much traffic congestion, considerate motorists would leave enough of a gap for vehicles wishing to turn into side streets from the other side of the road. From their position they would be unable to see anyone on a bike who is obscured by the stationary cars. Likewise, we are unable to see any cars turning into these side streets until the last second.

Luckily, I had changed my brake pads recently, as the way they had been a month ago would have meant a certain collision. For someone as useless as myself when it comes to any form of handywork, doing this on my own was a major achievement. I never fix anything on my bike, but eventually it reached the stage where I had no ability to slow down at all. The only options available were to buy a new bike or to change the brake pads, so after a few useful YouTube video lessons I challenged myself. For one of the rare times in life, I did so successfully.

The driver saw me far too late to be able to stop, and though she slammed on her brakes at the last second, it alone was too late. Only the simultaneous application of my brakes had prevented collision, though such was the severity of the stop that I had fallen from the bike. The driver held a hand up to apologise but I didn't blame her. It is the nature of the traffic flow at a spot like this. Other motorists are allowing them through and encouraging them to take the gap while it exists in such busy traffic. There is no way this lady could have seen me. Quite simply the only reason there was no accident was my readiness for it. Wherever my mind was, my eyes were in the right spot. My planning with the brake pads was in preparation for moments like this, which are inevitable at some point when you cycle in peak hour.

'Are you alright,' the lady asked after jumping straight out of her car after stopping in the side street. She was older than me and despite the fact I had copped the physical brunt of what had just happened, she seemed to have been more impacted than I had by the near collision.

'Yes, fine,' I said, acknowledging the nature of the situation being one that neither of us could do anything to avoid. It doesn't matter who is to blame, there is always a feeling of guilt that a driver will carry if they hit a cyclist. She double checked my welfare but following my insistence that all was well and seeing me prepare to take off again, she got back in her car and continued her journey.

It never makes sense to me how often these situations lead to road rage. Shit happens. As a cyclist, when you learn to take a more defensive approach, you get yourself out of trouble when it comes along. If someone intentionally wrongs you, fine; yell and kick and scream. Something like this was not a failure to look. Even if it was, my heart rate isn't going to be fixed by abusing her. What would the gain have been? Most likely the lesson she'd have driven off with, would have been *I should have hit that arsehole*. You achieve more in life by being the better person. She'll treat the next situation with even more care, so the road is that slight fraction safer for the nature of my response.

Given where my mind had been, this may have finally been my punishment for that Thursday in the park after school 30 years ago. More likely, for my inaction against Mr. Russo. Who knows if he ever paid a price for what he was getting up to? My heart rate was going at triple the normal rate from this scare. Maybe if my mind hadn't been back there, I may have spotted her fractionally sooner and stopped without it being close. Yes, I was partly ready, but accidents occur based on fractions of a second. I was aware enough to survive. Maybe if I was truly aware I'd have reached a controlled stop and avoided all danger.

After the quick exchange with the driver, I had looked back to Bus Stop 7 and the four people waiting to see if they'd noticed the commotion. I wondered if any of them would regale their colleagues or classmates about 'Lance Armstrong' having an accident just after he passed their bus stop. I don't bare any resemblance to Lance Armstrong but that doesn't matter. If all they know me as is someone who rides a bike past them each morning, then using my method in life they would surely have christened me with a name synonymous with bikes such as Armstrong's. I probably deserve the name of a fiend like him rather than someone remembered more heroically.

I guess most people don't quite operate like me. Maybe some people do. Maybe they had another more creative name for me. Maybe despite seeing me day after day I hadn't made enough impact on them to have any sense of recognition of me, the way I did for them. I feel like I fail to make an initial impact on too many people, at least not a favourable one.

I work in a building with a thousand other people, yet most of them pay no attention to anyone they haven't been forced into contact with. Every day you get in an elevator and see people almost strain their necks to ensure they don't make eye contact. To me it makes no sense to be acting like these people are strangers. We share life in a society. I may be anti-social and often try to avoid too much contact with anyone, but basic interaction seems normal. This seems to occur progressively less with time. People consider strangers should be avoided in every way, even though every person of value in their lives was at one point a stranger. It is the half-chance that people work with them, go to school with them or are part of the same club that has led to each of their friendships. People who may be more suitable friends may be the ones walking past them, or on a different floor of the building. This closed mindset is stopping people from finding their ideal networks. Escape to a small town and people understand society and interact. The bigger the city, the more they isolate. I have lived next to the same man for seven years and we've never had a conversation. It is so typical of city life in the 21st century.

The cities get more crowded yet there has never been more loneliness in the world.

Dogs see a new dog and go sniff each other's backsides. I'm not recommending that course of action, but most forms of life instinctively acknowledge similar beings, even if the interaction is minimal. We're straining to dodge what is natural, with our quest for outright avoidance.

Calming slowly, my heart rate was still more like at the end of a tough hill climb. The impact of the fear and panic outweigh the lack of exercise I had done to this point. This wasn't close enough to have my life flash before my eyes the way people speak about, but it still shook me sufficiently to have a physical and a psychological impact. If I'd been killed on the ride to work, so what. It really wasn't a consequence that concerned me, yet when you're not mentally prepared for the moment, you act on instinct. Instinct pushes survival above all else.

How ironic that this near miss should have happened with a car turning into Olive St. The impact on my heart would have been the same anywhere, but happening here adds an extra dimension to me. My grandmother's name was Olive, and it was after her that I named my daughter Olivia. Olivia was the greatest joy of my existence until such time as she became the greatest sorrow. The reason for living then the reason for no longer wanting to live.

I move on to the footpath and stop, fumbling through my backpack for a moment as I pretend to be looking for something just in case prying eyes are observing me. My focus really is just on regaining my composure. Eleven years have passed, but I cannot think of Olivia without slipping into an incomparable feeling of sadness. I can rarely go any time without thinking of her, but I've become accustomed over the years to quickly move from the worst moment to the best, smile and move on. The emotion of the moment with the near accident has sent me into these thoughts in a less controlled manner than normal. It takes an extra concerted effort to move on positively.

Nobody in Adelaide knows too much of the story. Once Dad died there was really nobody left here in terms of family. Most of my friends from my younger years lost touch with me through the period I was in Queensland. Although many of them were aware of Olivia and all that happened, they were far enough removed to feel sufficiently awkward not to bring things up. Most of my life since moving back to Adelaide has been around people I never previously knew. None of these people had any idea of my previous life. People ask if I have children and it is far easier to say no than to go into the full explanation of my past. I had a couple of years of supposed healing before I came back here. When I arrived, I was determined to be starting a new life. Maybe I should have gone somewhere else, but as much as there were skeletons here that I wanted to avoid, there was also the comfort of familiarity. I don't seek to hide or deny the story of Olivia, but I feel it's something to reserve for people I get to know on a deeper level than mere casual acquaintance.

Even after so many years there is no dulling of the images in my mind. The good and the bad I still see. Somehow, I seem to have developed the ability to focus on the positive when I'm in public. Rest assured there are few nights where I sleep soundly without the negative images from 2008 playing through my subconscious and disturbing me greatly. I don't know how I made it through the first twelve months but realistically I kept listening to the advice that told me it would get better. Eventually I learnt that this advice was bullshit. It never got better. Hearts may heal when they've been broken in many cases, but there is a whole other level of disintegration that they never recover from. Maybe it's not the size of the crisis that makes the difference and is more to do with the nature of the person. Maybe a stronger, better man would have overcome this all after a long enough time. Maybe the Anthony Speed that I was meant to be would have eventually been able to move on, but somewhere through the traumas of life he'd been suppressed into the Anthony Speed I actually am.

How much of ourselves is what nature has made us and how much of us is the experiences that we have? The nature versus nurture debate is inconclusive but I'm adamant that the sum of everything I have lived through has made me a very different person to what I would have been in different circumstances. I know that I carry certain characteristics of my late father, to ensure that I can't deny nature having a place. I maintain that certain facial features and a pun-based sense of humour define me substantially less than the traits which stem from all that I've endured.

As I return to the road cursing the 90 seconds I have lost, I see Olivia's face in my head, and I feel a little sense of comfort. Having been close enough to crashing a minute earlier it was not the time to get distracted, so I concentrate on the cars around me. Those heading my direction have advanced a little while the lights at the next intersection had been green, but it would take a couple more sequences for these cars to get through that bottleneck. Amazingly a strict focus on something has quickly got my mind in another place. My mind doesn't work in such a way that I can retain that focus, but at least when it moves it won't necessarily return to the past. Certain topics don't disappear as easily as others.

Walking up the footpath on the same side as me I see Lemon. I usually use more traditional names, but I was never able to find one that captured the sourness of her face as well as Lemon. Maybe Lemon is nothing like I suspect, but the term 'resting bitch face' appears to have been designed specifically for her. Day after day I pass her and there is never anything but the sourest expression on her face. I've sometimes joked to myself that she is the poster-girl for children who pulled a face when the wind changed. I figure she looks like I generally feel so I shouldn't be so judgemental. I can't help but wonder why she doesn't take the first step. At least try not to look like the saddest person on Earth.

What makes her that way? Who am I kidding? What has made *me* this way? So many distinct factors have combined to slowly kill me on the inside. If the outside reflected the inside, I would look far sourer than Lemon, who might not be sour at all. I'm intrigued enough that I would really like to know more about her, but how? Not only is it not the way of our society to initiate conversation with random strangers, but it is also a practical impossibility. I'm riding one way while she is walking another. This is our only interaction. If I stopped and pulled up alongside her I'm sure she would feel intimidated. Nothing would be achieved. If I knew her name, I could try and find her on social media to learn a little, but I won't get far searching under 'Lemon.'

I used to enjoy social media, but I have found with time that it drains and depresses me. It saddened me to be ignored, it bothered me to be disagreed with and yet there was no positive payoff to compensate for the negatives. Why expose yourself to situations where the set of potential results are all negative? I go to work each day knowing that I'm destined for a range of negative elements, but every fortnight my payslip reminds me why I am there. Social media doesn't have an equivalent payoff. Nobody cares what anyone else thinks, but everyone loves to hear their own thoughts expressed by others. People seek validation, for themselves and their opinions. An incoherent ramble of a popular opinion will achieve this. A thorough and well reasoned argument for an unpopular opinion will be berated. Nothing is achieved, and the popularity contest continues to follow its predetermined progress. The positives of social media are insignificant, but the negatives have a real impact. Maybe it's just me reading an unhealthy amount into everything but I am glad I deleted all of my social media accounts a few years ago.

Oh well, credit where it is due. Lemon has got me away from focusing on Olivia and the guaranteed downward spiral I would have been heading in. Given a chance I decide that I'd give Lemon a squeeze. No, I think she might leave a sour taste in my mouth. I have a quick chuckle, my mood temporarily enhanced a little, and continue on.

CHAPTER 12

TUESDAY MARCH 10, 2015

'Do you have any questions for the panel?'

The interview had gone reasonably well. There was no reason why it shouldn't. I was somewhat overqualified for the position and with my experience and knowledge, I'd had every reason to feel confident. Despite this, any situation where I was being evaluated left me nervous. The justifiable confidence I should have felt was most likely well hidden from the panel. The thought that they would notice my nerves had only made these worse. Momentum shapes moments, and thankfully getting a good answer across early in the interview had shifted the momentum my way.

The interview was being conducted by Terry, Madeleine and Patrick. They were all team leaders in the branch. While I had a positive feeling from Madeleine and Patrick, Terry, who was chairing the panel, was a different story.

'How long have you all worked here?' I asked. It is always important to ask questions even though I didn't have anything I felt I needed them to tell me. Part of the preparation for any interview was learning what I needed to. For a job like this, what I learnt was more than what I needed to know, thus the questions were just a futile part of the process that only occasionally delivered the best candidate into a job.

'Five years for me, about the same for Patrick, and about three years for you isn't it, Madeleine?' Terry said.

'Yes, just over three.'

'So, there are opportunities to advance reasonably quickly?' I said more as a comment than a follow-up question.

'Look, the job is as advertised. If you are looking for a leadership role then you should apply for that,' Terry said curtly. It seemed like a valid question to me. I was more than happy to be in the position on offer, but I didn't want to spend forever under people that I was more qualified than. It wasn't so much the substance of the answer that concerned me, but the abrasive style of its delivery.

'It hasn't always been structured to allow career progression, but as an organisation we have really sought to improve that. There is much better development of staff and more opportunities on offer,' Patrick said.

The panel weren't contradicting each other yet also didn't seem completely unified. They may have been trying to paint the same picture, but they were using different sets of colours to do so.

'We all started at the bottom when there were far less options,' Madeleine said. 'I would probably not still be here without the changes that have been made, but I'm glad that I am. It is a great organisation to be a part of.'

An interview always feels best when the panel is selling the organisation to you rather than you as the candidate having to do the sales job. I guess I had done my part well enough in response to their formal questions, at least for two of the panel. Terry still needed more convincing.

'Can I ask you, why do you want a job that you are clearly over-qualified for?'

It is dangerous to make judgements about anyone too quickly, but maybe he and I were both doing that with each other. My hatred of conflict sometimes led me down that path. Maybe insecurity drove him in a similar manner. Possibly he saw my experience and thought that I would be leadership potential, and a threat to his career progress. Of course, there may be any number of other reasons for it, but his approach to the interview seemed to be combative. I'd never struck it quite so directly in an interview before. So much of the way through, I had to direct my eye contact with the other two on the panel, as every look at Terry had me feeling under attack, his dark eyes honing in on me uncomfortably. The other two provided the reassurance that I was performing well.

I kept the chatter about the changes in the branch going, less in the quest of answers and more intrigued now by Terry's attitude in response.

'If staff are rotated regularly, does it have an impact on team dynamics?'

'No, I haven't seen any indication of that,' Madeleine said. 'Mind you, it is a period of transition, and it is something that we as a management group are mindful of.'

'You would have issues with rotation?' Terry asked.

'Certainly not. It provides the opportunity to learn and experience more, so it is good individually but it also no doubt provides added flexibility to the workplace. Seems very much like an everybody wins result.' I could envisage a whole lot of negatives as well, but this wasn't the time or place to be discussing them. I read the panel well enough to know that two people would be ensuring I was hired. Terry would love to reject me, but under the process they had to follow, he would find grounds to do so impossible.

Interviews are like first dates. Both sides are always trying to make the best possible impression on the other. Years ago, I let my colleague Zoe set me up with her friend, believing she was talking about the beautiful Anna. To my disappointment, it turned out to be Charlene, the most uninteresting woman I had ever met. While honesty may be the best policy, it also seemed the hardest. I went along on a first date with Charlene with a clear plan. I did everything possible to make a bad impression, resolute in my aim of encouraging her to reject me. We didn't have a second date, so technically my plan worked, but it also saw my reputation crushed with Zoe. Now with a low opinion of me, she ensured that Anna never heard a good word about me.

It seemed to me that this interview was similar. Terry had taken my role, casting me in the role of Charlene. I was meant to walk away certain I didn't want the job. If he'd conducted the interview on his own, that may have worked. I had nobody to redeem my date with Charlene, but Patrick and Madeleine had destroyed his plan by showing me that the workplace would be far better than what Terry was portraying.

I haven't worked full-time since moving back to Adelaide. While I thought the gaps in my resume would be a drawback, it was easily explained away during the interview. The job hadn't sounded interesting on paper, but there seemed to be enough diversity to the functions that it could hold interest for a while. I wasn't looking for the ideal job, just for something to get me back into a routine. From there, finding the right job would be far easier. I felt it looked the ideal place to work for six months or so.

What if Terry ended up as my team leader? I'm sure he wasn't so bad. Most likely I'd be in another area anyway. Worst case scenario, he becomes my boss, and he is as bad as I fear. For a few months, how difficult can that really be. It is not like I'm going to be staying for years.

CHAPTER 13

8.30am

There are two major intersections I deal with each morning, and at these points I really appreciate being on a bike rather than stuck in a car. I can fit in the smallest gaps or go up on to the footpath as necessary. At this point of the journey, I spend more time moving and less time waiting than most. Paying less attention than normal has seen me get trapped at the red light behind a couple of cars as we wait to turn left. The one immediately in front of me is a Mercedes-Benz. Every time I'm stuck beside or behind one of these for long, I know where my mind will end up. The car is largely irrelevant, but it serves as a reminder of one of the darkest days of my life. It may seem self-absorbed to consider this to be about me when it really is the story of others, but every part of life interconnects. No story belongs to any person without having an impact and a flow-on effect for other people.

If my life was a movie, then I would be the star. My family and friends would be supporting cast, absent from the current scene where all the people at this intersection would be extras. If any of their lives were a movie, then *I* would be the extra. Either way, we're all appearing on the same screen. If something dramatic enough happens here in the next few seconds, it will impact not just the star, but the supporting cast and extras too. The Mercedes I remember may have been pivotal to an early turning point in the film of my life, but it's place in the films of a few other lives carried even greater significance.

I was six years old when we moved into the house of my father's dreams. It wasn't the most amazing house, but it was in one of the most impressive streets in town. Given its poor condition when we bought it, a lot of work was needed and as a result it was priced at a level that dad could manage.

There was a park across the road from home, and for all the local kids, this park became the centre of our universe. As a shy kid, I was less likely to be seen there than most others, often preferring to play alone in the backyard. More than anything it was the influence of my siblings that forced me out across the road and usually I'd follow them hanging around with some of the older kids from the neighbourhood.

There were enough kids in the street to ensure that in time you would have no problems meeting friends. Vanessa and Tom knew some of our neighbours from school. Across the road was a family with four kids that had a similar age range to us. I didn't bond so well with any of them and spent more time with our neighbour Ben. He regularly bowled to me on our made-up cricket pitch in the park. A couple of years older than me, the pace he bowled at really prepared me for what I would face at school.

Further up the street was an annoying kid named Craig. He was the only kid in the street who didn't go to one of the two closest schools. He rarely hung out in the park with the rest of the kids from our street, preferring to spend his time with a different group of kids from his own school. I was more than happy to not think of him as part of our street. Opposite Craig's house lived the O'Connor's, and it was these kids that I ended up building the closest friendships with.

The regally named Edward, William and Arthur lived in the house most would refer to as the best house in the best street. They were distant cousins of mine, not that I knew it until many years later. I never worked out the exact connection, but their mother Anne was related through my maternal grandmother. Grandma did one day explain the relationship, but it was distant enough to not mean much to me. Essentially, they were my friends and nothing else mattered.

Edward was a year younger than me and was the first real best friend I'd ever had. Riding our bikes, kicking the football or anything else that took our fancy, we became continually more inseparable with time. Although we were at separate schools, we were already excited for the next school year. In Year 3, Edward would be moving to my school. Not that our parents were keen on the idea, but we had already committed that we would ride to school together. While we'd obviously not be in the same classes, we figured expanding our times together was ideal enough. It was probably guaranteed to be the one and only time I would ever look ahead at the start of a school year with more enthusiasm than the end of the previous one.

William was two years younger. We probably looked more like brothers than either of us resembled our siblings. The chubby cheeks and curly blonde hair meant people who didn't know better, often considered Edward the odd one out. In some ways William seemed more like an eldest child than Edward. While the older boy tended to follow me around like a lost puppy, William was more inclined to make his own decisions. When he needed to lead, he would serve as the boy in charge of his baby brother, while when it suited, he would blend in with Edward and me with no issues. Arthur had just turned three and as much as he struggled to keep up with us at times, he made sure he was never too far from being part of things. My life may have been primarily about Edward and me, but our group of four was tight enough. The park across the road may well have been our own, such was the amount of time we could be found there all together.

Despite living in the same well-to-do street there was a significant socio-economic divide between the two households. The O'Connor's lived there because they belonged there, while we were there through my father's desire to present an image, accurate or not. Our house was his way of showing the world he'd made it, while the debilitating mortgage hid in the background. As a child I wasn't aware of this, but I do remember the differences that existed within the two houses. The other kids had the best of everything. I never wanted for anything, but it was always kept within reason. I didn't want every toy under the sun, and had simple tastes. I had a cricket bat, a tennis racquet, a football and a bike, but in each case it was a much cheaper version than what the O'Connor boys had. It didn't matter to me, for in each case it was everything I needed. Compared with most kids I was spoiled but compared with the O'Connor's, I was living in squalor, not that I realised. Children are incredibly impressionable, and the dynamics of our group saw me as the eldest be the primary influence. My lack of enthusiasm for their latest toys meant that in time they were happiest shunning those things and focusing on going with my choices. As such we spent vast amounts of time on our bikes. When we'd had enough of that, the two younger boys would generally leave Edward and me to the other sporting options that we'd continue as a duo.

One day Edward and I were in the backyard at my house kicking the football to each other. One of Edwards kicks went almost straight up in the air. I knew that as he'd kicked it my job was to mark it. Unfortunately, he figured as it was closest to him it meant he should mark it. Both of us sprinted with our eyes on the ball before colliding with my front teeth planted into his forehead. I did severe damage to my teeth while Edward was bleeding profusely. Paranoid at the sight of blood I was more worried by what I saw than what I felt. My mother was more panicked again at the sight of the carnage in the backyard. Within moments she had me booked in for emergency dental work. All the while I continued to cry out. 'What about Edward.'

'He just needs a band-aid,' Mum said.

He had managed to run home of his own accord. What his mother thought of the dangers of her little boy hanging around with that dangerous kid from number three was un-certain, but I still felt worse about his wound than mine. The headaches that both of us felt kept us off our feet for the next day, but by the weekend the two of us, with his two brothers in tow were exactly as we had been before.

The O'Connor's had a holiday home on the Yorke Penin-sular and were heading over there for the Easter break which coincided with the first week of the school holidays. I was so excited to be going with them until out hopes were quashed. I should have known it couldn't happen as we were having a family holiday on the Gold Coast, but at eight years old, working out the exact dates of these things wasn't my job. I had assumed, or just hoped, that the two trips wouldn't clash, but unfortunately that wasn't the case.

With great disappointment I said goodbye to the boys for a week and a half on the Wednesday afternoon. They would be on their way the following morning and wouldn't be back until the following week. Before that time, we'd be off to Queensland for one wonderful week. I was happier to be going there. It was the longest flight I'd ever been on, and it seemed like such an exciting place to be going, but I did accept that I was going to be missing an amazing trip with the boys.

After the dull loneliness of Thursday and Friday, I was so excited when Saturday arrived. It was destined to be a long day as we weren't flying until the afternoon. We'd packed and prepared in every way before the day so that Dad could still work in the morning and Tom and Vanessa could go to tennis. For me, the day would no doubt end with great excitement but was guaranteed to be dull and uninteresting until then.

Never take for granted what a day has in store.

CHAPTER 14

SATURDAY MAY 12, 1984

I have been looking forward to today for so long. This afternoon my Mum and Dad, Tom, Vanessa and I are flying to the Gold Coast for a week's holiday. I have been on a plane before, but never this far. It is so exciting, but it does feel kind of strange right now because it's still so many hours until we leave. I don't know what to do with myself.

I spend most of my time with my best friend Edward, and a lot of the time his two younger brothers William and Arthur. They already left on their holiday with their Mum on Thursday, so I can't go and see them. I was about to go up to their place before I remembered they'd gone. It shouldn't be so hard to forget, for their family invited me to go with them. If we didn't have the trip to the Gold Coast happening, then I would be at their shack with them right now.

Dad, Vanessa, and Tom are all out now, so it is just Mum and me home. All the packing was done yesterday so there's nothing to do. They will all be home around lunchtime, and we don't leave home until about 4pm, so it's a long, boring day until then.

While I'm away I won't be riding my bike. I never normally go a day without riding at least a little bit, so I take the opportunity to hop on. I don't have anywhere to go, so I decide I will just ride the regular pathway around the house and up to the front gate then down the driveway. I imagine sometimes that it's a car racing circuit and the little path near the side of the house is pit lane where I can pull in when I need some variety after enough laps. I love car racing. I love cars. I can't wait until I can drive.

As I get to the front gate on one of my laps, I see Craig and a couple of his friends walking down the street. My normal inclination would be to ride to the back of the house and get off the bike, so they didn't see me. In the imaginary race in my head, there are only a couple of laps left, so I decided to continue as normal and just hope that the boys walk straight past and ignore me.

'That's so sad about the O'Connor's,' Craig said.

'What is?'

'They're dead. All of them except Mr. O'Connor. Killed in a car crash. Didn't you know?'

For a moment I stared blankly at him. Tears were forming in my eyes but didn't quite fall due to the uncertainty of their reason. Should I be crying that Craig would make up something like this or should I be crying because this had actually happened. I said nothing and rode to the back of the house and ran inside the backdoor screaming.

'MUM,' I screamed, running until finding her on the phone. She hung up, aware of what I must have learnt.

'Craig says the O'Connor's are dead from a car crash,' I yelled as the tears were now falling. 'Is it true.'

Mum was now starting to cry as she picked me up and hugged me.

'I'm so sorry Anthony.'

I've never known anyone who has died. My grandfathers are both dead, but they died before I was born. The boys can't be dead, they're younger than me. It doesn't make sense how something like this can happen.

My mum explains that they didn't want me to know until the end of our holiday as they wanted me to enjoy it. That made sense, but it seemed wrong to keep secrets like this. Mum and Dad always tell me not to keep secrets. They never then say its ok provided it's helping someone have a better holiday.

I remember back to Thursday night. Every night Dad rushes to make sure the TV is on the news at 6pm. If we have to be somewhere else, he tries to make sure it's after the news. On Thursday when the news started, he ran to the TV to turn it off. The accident must have been on there. They thought I'd recognise the car, so they tried to keep it hidden from me. It's strange that all of this didn't get me curious, but without seeing the story I never would have contemplated any of it. How could I contemplate something so impossible to imagine?

I ran to my bedroom crying. Mum came and did all she could to try and console me. When Dad got home, he tried the same thing. So too did my siblings when they returned. Everyone had known and kept it from me. Nothing could make me feel any better. Nothing could help me to understand how and why such a thing could happen. Nothing could make me understand how I could ever feel like anyone could be guaranteed to come home again whenever they went out. My heart was ripped out and nothing made sense anymore.

Today was meant to be the most wonderful day but now it is a disaster. I know that soon we will have a taxi arrive to pick us up and take us to the airport. I said I didn't want to go anymore but have been told I have no choice.

'I know nothing can make things feel better right now Anthony,' Mum said on yet another attempt at raising my mood a little. 'Life isn't fair. None of us ever learn why the saddest things can happen to the best people. When something so sad happens, it is alright to cry, to be sad and to feel how wrong it is, but we can't let it take over. You don't make anything better by staying here crying all week. When we go away you will still feel sad, tonight, tomorrow, Monday, and so on, but at least each day you will see that a few extra things will happen to make you smile, to make you feel better just for a little while. That is all that we can do. Smile when we can and remember the smiles of those boys. Don't just cry about missing them, smile about how special they were to you while they were here.'

I was incapable of agreeing or giving any sort of positive feedback, though at least in that moment she could see I'd listened and accepted her words a little.

I close my eyes and remember the boys smiling and laughing and for a moment I smile before bursting into tears again. Maybe life isn't what we think it is. I start to think that if such tragedy is just part of living then maybe the boys are blessed to escape in this way. I'm only at that point for a moment before Vanessa comes in and tells me that going away now is the best thing possible.

'You might be sad the whole time, but it's better to be crying away from here. Do you really want the kids up the street hanging around talking about it to you? Do you want to see Mr. O'Connor every day right now?'

She was right. Getting away wasn't to enjoy the destination, it was to escape. Running away from what I really didn't want to face. Maybe when things are bad, running away and escaping is the best option.

CHAPTER 15

8.32AM

The sadness I felt wasn't a reaction to the tragedy that would disappear with time. Here I am riding to work forty years later, and I have tears in my eyes at the memory. The fact that I am riding and not driving isn't a coincidence. The car has always been a source of angst for me since that day. I learnt to drive in my teens but never felt comfortable in the driver's seat. I failed to get my licence and then after learning again twenty years later, I still didn't end up taking the next step.

I felt a sadness in the pit of my stomach every time that I saw Mr. O'Connor across the years that we continued to live on the same block. How could he not be reminded of his sons every time he saw me? Surely I was a painful reminder of his loss. I felt guilty, not that I had a reason to, but it felt unfair that he should have to see me grow up in front of his eyes. With each stage of my development, he'd have been reminded of how it should be for Edward, William and Arthur. Nothing about the lives and deaths of these boys and their mother made sense to anyone, most certainly not a child. After all these years, it's a rarer focus, yet still no easier to accept.

I don't know too much about the accident. When I heard about it, I was far too scarred to be looking into details. The tragedy was all that mattered in a situation like this. The where's, why's and how's just don't matter. With time the desire to know more has grown but the ability to find out those details has become tougher. I believe that Anne was speeding, and I think she had briefly taken her eyes off the road, most likely to look back at the boys and tell them off. Would such a thing have happened if I was with them? An extra person in the car, someone having to sit in the front seat. Could my presence have made a difference? Would the accident have been avoided? Would I too have been killed? At the age of eight, I wasn't asking these questions. The accident spurned nothing but grief. Once the worst of this passed, the thoughts of the accident transitioned from emotion to philosophy. Decades later, I understand it no better, yet continue these reflections regularly.

I've always hated speeding vehicles since that time. I never cared what people's excuses were, it was never cool or macho to me to see someone flouting road rules. When you've lost people in circumstances like these, your views have to change. Speeding is never too relevant in the peak hour traffic I endure on the way to work, but you can see the impatience in drivers, and you know where that sort of attitude can lead to.

The light goes green, but a red left arrow remains while pedestrians cross Glen Osmond Road and I curse again at being stuck in this spot. It may sound kind of hypocritical to blame others for their impatience, but I validate mine by saying that I'm not going to be killing anyone if I start going too fast. As if I could go too fast these days for anything. Speed isn't just a theoretical enemy of mine, but a practical impossibility given my lack of physical fitness. I may be Speed by name, but no word was a less suitable description of me.

Outside of my immediate family, the people in my life have changed continually over the years. Circumstances ensure that happens to some extent for most people. Some friendships survive, but changes in school, job, residence, and the like usually led to people drifting apart and establishing new relationships with other people. On that basis the prospects that the boys and I would have had lifelong friendships is unlikely, yet I feel as though Edward and I had a special connection that would have lasted. I imagine us as teens, as young adults and at the current point of life. I imagine him as a 45-year-old man today. I imagine him having children and that I would be the godfather to them. Every time I think of these stages I not only imagine the man that never had the chance to live, but I see my own life in such a different way.

Where would I be if that accident didn't happen? There's every chance I wouldn't be turning into Glen Osmond Road right now on my bike. I probably would drive. That may be only a small part of life, but it highlights the domino effect that occurs. One event triggers so much more. I probably wouldn't be in my current dead-end job. I would have been more sociable, more confident, more outgoing and a different person for it. All of those characteristics would have sent me in different directions from the age of eight. Ever beyond, I would have been far more likely to live to my potential.

The deaths of Edward and his brothers didn't cause every negative in my life. There is always a way of getting past every moment and changing the future. No one event seals your future destiny, but it can point you in a direction. My own weakness meant that once pointed in the wrong direction, I allowed myself to keep headed that way. That isn't the result of the O'Connor tragedy. I own that.

As I've done many thousands of times before, I ride on, the thoughts of Edward, his brothers and his mother in my head. With time I can't help but wonder the purity of the memories. Do I remember the moments, or do I remember the memory of the moments? Our memories are not perfect, and so events that we recall tend to evolve ever so slightly in our minds. All of that is insignificant compared with the big issues that the tragedy highlights. Any day could be our last. Life happens around us controlled by millions of different forces. Sometimes we win, sometimes we lose, and fairness is irrelevant. All we can do is learn from what we experience and put the odds in our favour when we can. Despite the opportunities, I never seem to have learnt the right lessons from this saga. For all the dwelling I had done on the O'Connor family, there was one member I really should have been learning from.

CHAPTER 16

THURSDAY FEBRUARY 7, 2018

He lived 70 years. 25,500 days. 613,000 hours. 37 million minutes. 2.2 billion seconds. All those insignificant moments that combine to make a life, yet all of them are overshadowed by just one moment. One fleeting instant, when everything that his life was built upon was taken away from him.

Matthew O'Connor was a tragic figure. How do you go on after losing your wife and three children so suddenly? It has always been beyond my comprehension as to how he managed to rebuild his life so successfully.

Matthew continued to live in the same house. The reminders of all he had lost were in front of him each day. The double story house on the corner that I had previously spent so much time in, has always looked haunted to me since. I imagined him walking from one empty room to the next. Time standing still, the pain never leaving.

I would have run far away. Having done it, I've learnt how pathetically ineffective it is. Running away is easy, but you never run fast enough to escape the problems. However far you run, they catch you and retain their hold. Staying and facing the problems is much harder in the short term, but once you overcome the painstaking requirements of recovery, you can conquer them.

I gave up smoking. Forty-seven times I gave up smoking. Forty-six times I started again. In most attempts at quitting, I was fine so long as I didn't have cigarettes around me. Naturally, the opportunity eventually arose, and every time, I fell apart. I'd run away from an addiction, but I wasn't truly escaping it. The addiction was only truly conquered once I had reached the stage of staying and facing it. Once opportunity could be constant, yet temptation didn't accompany it, then success has been reached.

Matthew faced tragedy at a level most people could never contemplate. To lose one person, so young and so suddenly is hard to recover from. To lose all four of your family in such a way defies thought. He'd lost everything, at least in my eyes. Somehow, he stayed in the game. He rebuilt his life.

I hadn't seen him in twenty years, but something made me feel I needed to be here. I had never really known him, yet we were intrinsically linked by the same moment. When he lost everything, I lost comparatively little, yet both our lives were shaped to an extent on that day. So much of what has happened through my life stemmed from the pain of that day, and more significantly my inability to overcome it.

Matthew died a week ago from a sudden heart attack, having apparently been in good health. It was pure chance that I ran into a former neighbour on Monday who had told me about his passing. I found the funeral notice in the paper. The church was crowded with people wishing to commemorate his life, though not a face I recognised was amongst them.

I'd often thought of him. A symbol of resilience. A source of admiration. A reminder of how different people can be in the manner they face situations. Being aware of this was one thing. Doing something about it isn't so easy.

The service was enlightening. He remarried a little over a decade later. He had no more children, but he did manage to have a love that lasted and provided some of what he'd lost. He was successful professionally and was fulfilled in other parts of life. Obviously, he would never have lived a day without the thoughts of what might have been and should have been. While most people would parlay those losses, Matthew ensured that the impact of the tragedy on his life did not increase with time. I seem to have failed dismally on that score. I ensure that every tragedy I've lived through not only impacted me at the time, but led to further issues and growing costs going forward.

How different is the truth to what is seen by the rest of the world? Maybe we were presented today with a picture of Matthew that kept the pain hidden. If I died today, what would people say of my life. Would they say that I overcame the tragedy and rebuilt a happy life, or do they see the real me?

CHAPTER 17

8.33AM

On the left-hand side of the road is a business named Harris Carpets. A simple enough business, but its name was almost guaranteed to see me jump from one of life's tragedies to another. As certain as time hadn't helped me forget the O'Connor's, nearly thirty-five years hadn't begun to diminish the effect of the Harris name on me.

When you look back with the benefit of hindsight things can look so obvious. It can be impossible to work out how they were missed at the time. How did I not understand what was happening? How did the school allow this to happen? How did nobody else see what was going on? I don't believe that this could occur today. In the 1980's the world was sufficiently different in many ways that people's eyes were closed to certain things.

Mr. Harris was a contradiction in many ways. As coach of the school football team, he had an aura of masculinity that highlighted his strength as a male role model. As the school drama teacher, he presented a different, more cultured side, but this didn't seem to draw away from the strong male image.

He was the son of a prominent and successful man who had served as the mayor of his local area for over two decades. The father had been a migrant, arriving in Australia as a child. He had overcome a tough upbringing to be a true success story. He'd provided a much better life for his children, four daughters and one son. On the surface the son appeared to have inherited much of his father's character. With the additional opportunities that were afforded to him, the expectations he would have faced through life were significant.

While he hadn't been a star on the football field he was heavily involved with his local club as an administrator and volunteer, following in the footsteps of his father who was a former chairman and life member. He had decided to become a primary school teacher, a profession that a man could choose in the 1970's without standing out. I expect it was likely to be considered falling short of the hopes that his ambitious father would have set for him. He would have liked a son who studied law before entering the political realm.

A man being single in his thirties wasn't unusual enough to arouse suspicion, but it was one of many signposts. When enough of these all point in one direction, it doesn't take an overly abstract mindset to start considering all the possibilities. Apparently in that era, people had a sufficiently naïve and trusting nature that they didn't draw the right conclusions.

What makes someone like this so evil, is not so much their instinctive impulses, nor even their unforgivable actions. The worst aspect is the calm and calculating way they work on satisfying their sick fantasies. It didn't begin in any way that a child could have perceived as wrong. It was a long-term strategy designed to gain trust and then build on this, simultaneously infiltrating their life in different ways. Every tiny step would seem like a normal progression. It was just the same way that the game plan of the football team got built. The same principle as our school drama production had developed from reading lines, to a full staged production. Just as Mr. Harris pulled these strings, he moved from being a nurturing friendly leader to a sadistic molester without any of his victims having a clue what was happening. When people hear stories like these, they always focus on the details at the end, but it is this process of premeditation that is the defining example of their evil.

Over the years, the more I look back, the earlier I can see the tell-tale signs first appeared. From the moment the group walked into his classroom on the first day of the school year, he was working us out. Who were the most vulnerable children? Who would be easiest to prey on? Who had the biggest self-esteem issues? I don't think he cared about appearances, he was focused on opportunity. The child that kept secrets, the child that was insecure, the child that displayed the most fear, the child that most needs attention. That is the combination that the sickest predator looks to target. That child will appreciate the first bits of attention most. That child will offer the least resistance to any suggestion you put in his head. That child will be the least likely to ever say a word. I was that child. Or should I say I was one of those children, as I can never know how many other victims he had.

At the end of the year, he took a group of four of us away to his beachside holiday house. Safety in numbers, our parents would all have thought. Of course, it now seems strange that a teacher would be associating with his now former students during school holidays. Then, if anyone was offering a few days of fun at the beach for their child then it seemed reasonable. When it's a known trusted professional, what harm could there be? They would all have viewed it as nothing to worry about, as having those other kids there would ensure the security of each of their sons.

There was not a semblance of any sort of inappropriate behaviour, or at least nothing that I saw and can remember. I'm sure that the trip was mainly just an opportunity to further build his profile on each of us. Which parents reacted most curiously to this invitation? Which child seemed the odd one out in various scenarios? If he hadn't been certain of who his primary target from this year group was before this trip, he certainly was afterwards.

I barracked for a different football team to his, but sure enough he had the contacts to get me tickets to see my team play in the finals. He picked me up and took me home with absolutely nothing untoward in his conduct in any way. As my team had won, my memories of the day were incredibly positive, so saying yes to the next invitation seemed reasonable.

My parents marriage had recently ended, and the issues related to that may have been their primary focus at this time. They were aware of Mr. Harris showing me attention, but they knew he was a respectable man and that any involvement he'd had in my life had been positive and constructive. They knew his father. They believed that it could only be good for me to have an additional positive adult role model. I had seemed to be struggling with school in the past year despite having been accepted into Mensa as a high IQ child. They'd seen several ways in which I'd been withdrawing from other things I'd previously enjoyed.

My brother had moved to Melbourne several years ago to study and had lived with my uncle and aunt. After graduating, he had moved to London, and at this point of life he seemed a distant memory. My sister had moved to Tasmania with her boyfriend the previous year, and now my mother had left the state as well, moving to Brisbane. My best friends were killed in a car crash. Most of my other friends had disappeared from my life one way or another. It had felt at that stage like anyone in my life was only there out of force. Stuart Harris was the one exception. The one person who chose to be in my life. I knew enough to know I didn't want him there, yet he was skilled and manipulative enough to play through my weaknesses.

When he invited me to stay overnight at his home for the first time, it was under the pretence of watching the Wimbledon final. I was not to be the only other child there, so again, safety in numbers. It had been my birthday the week before, and I had got a new ten-speed racing bike. I would rather have stayed home and gone riding, but I struggled to say no to people and accepted his invitation.

Despite what I'd been told, it was just Mr. Harris there with me. We watched the tennis, just as he had said. It was the early hours of the morning when it finished, so naturally it would have been unreasonable to take me home then. There was plenty of room at his house. The spare room wasn't required as he had set up a blanket and pillows on the floor in front of the TV. I fell asleep but woke up later in the night with his arm around me and his crotch pressed firmly against my backside. I was petrified and didn't know what to say or do so I pretended to be asleep. I didn't go close to falling back asleep for the rest of the night. I am certain he knew I had woken up. He didn't say a word, either then or in the morning, but I think he knew how scared I was and that his best option was to leave it at that step.

I can only speculate, but other weekends he probably had other boys there. Each would be at various stages of his grooming process. He'd know what he could get away with and would plan the night accordingly. Eventually, it was my turn again. He knew my profile well enough, and that whether I would want to or not, I wouldn't be capable of saying no to any reasonable request. After saying I was unavailable one time, I ended up saying yes to spending another night at his house a couple of months later.

On the way to his place, we stopped for dinner at a fast-food place that he would have considered a treat for me. Given the diet that both dad and I shared, this was far more of a normal meal than a treat. What did make it different was the company and the conversation that it entailed. He told me about the funeral of David Wallace. Apparently one kid yelled abuse at him and said that it was his fault David had killed himself.

'How awful that people could make up such lies,' he said.
'What lies?' I asked.

'They said I'd hurt him. Done something bad. Naturally if I hurt children I wouldn't still be teaching,' he said.

Looking back, I find it curious that he would have outed himself as the bad guy, but he did. Although he referred to 'lies,' the very acknowledgement that people had claimed he was responsible for a teenager's suicide was significant. True or not, he was admitting that there was at least a perception that he was guilty of wrongdoing. That alone was enough to prove to me that this was not a situation I wanted to be in.

David had been two years older than me, and well past the age that Mr Harris taught, so the accusations were nothing to do with his teaching. I knew full well that his reference was that David had gone through the same experiences as I was now doing. It seemed to me that Mr. Harris was implying that anything I was ever to say about events would be lies and misinterpretations. I needed to learn to appreciate that his attention was a gift. Clearly David hadn't, and his fate was partially due to spreading 'lies.' He wanted me to learn that anything I said about what happened between us could only lead to bad things. Not for him, for me.

When we got back to his house, we watched a couple of movies that we had hired from the video store. After all these years the only things I remember about the movie *Jumping Jack Flash* are the title song and the predator who was watching me watch it. I can't even recall the second movie, probably as I was already focused on the fears of what would follow. At its end, he did the same routine of laying a makeshift bed on the floor in front of the TV, then pretending to fall asleep as his arm went around me. This time I never got to sleep. This time his arm didn't just hang around me, but his hand started working over my body. I tried to roll over to a point on my stomach so he couldn't reach down the front of my pyjama pants, but this then had him reaching under my pyjamas to touch my backside. I rolled further, all the time pretending to be asleep. He followed, and eventually his hand reached its next target, albeit outside of my pyjamas. Before long, his hand was down the front of my pants.

For many years I refused to accept what happened from here on in. It was only after years of reading and investigating that I found it was common for rape and assault victims to experience physical arousal in these situations, despite a feeling of fear and horror at what was happening. I did. I came in his hand. What I felt at the time was terror. What followed it was shame.

I was a naïve child. In the moment I was embarrassed. I pretended to suddenly wake up. I ran to the bathroom to clean up. I came back and he pretended to be asleep. I tried to get back in the bed as far away as I could be from him, but he wasn't going to leave me any space. The charade continued. I would pretend to be asleep due to fear, he would pretend to be asleep as an alibi if I confronted him.

He made a comment in the morning about how it was great having me stay there. He also said he was sure that I had felt good staying there too. Again, he knew exactly how far to push without going too far. He knew I wouldn't say no, but I also wasn't going to say yes. A former teacher at our school, Mr. Mooney had arrived at the house to see him about something. Unlike Mr. Harris, Mr. Mooney didn't have the same macho image. He was exactly the type all of us kids thought would be more inclined to want to share a bed with a boy. Mr. Harris told me I should go and have a shower which I did. I locked the door knowing what Mr. Harris was, and suspecting Mr. Mooney was there for the same reason. Whether there was a hole in a wall, or a video recorder set up I will never know. Maybe Mr. Mooney appearing out of the blue was coincidental and irrelevant. Either way, no teacher could possibly arrive at a colleague's house early in the morning, see a child had spent the night there and then not pass that information on. His inaction will always leave me thinking he was complicit.

As an adult it is easy to look back and question why I didn't speak out and ask for help. It is like being stranded in a foreign land, with no ability to understand the language spoken around you. I didn't understand any of this. I blamed myself for being in the position. I was overcome with fear. Fear of him. Fear of the reactions of everyone else for me being so stupid. Fear of what would happen if I let him continue, but fear of what would happen if I did anything to stop him. Would I end up like David Wallace?

I could only see one truth at that time. I was less the victim of an evil man than I was the victim of being an ignorant little boy. I couldn't face people knowing that. I constantly made excuses to avoid situations, but I could never say an outright no to him. I made excuses to avoid three different invitations for sleepovers, which clearly demonstrated my unwillingness to proceed, but he wasn't seeking consent.

He knew my profile. He knew he could wear me down. He knew I was too scared. Finally, he caught me off guard and I was trapped into another night at his house after a school concert.

CHAPTER 18

SATURDAY NOVEMBER 3, 1990

I don't know whether my hatred is greater towards him for what he is doing or myself for allowing him to do it. Either way, I refuse to allow this to ever happen again. I should never have let it happen this time or last time, yet I was too weak to say no.

Last night there was a concert at school. I had no reason to be there but for the fact that Daniel is in the school band and had encouraged me to come. I wasn't doing anything else, so I went along.

Mr. Harris heard that I was going, and then invited me to come over to his place afterwards. Usually, I'm set with excuses why I couldn't, but coming straight after I had said I'd be at the concert, I couldn't come up with anything. I should have said I was staying at Daniel's. I just wasn't ready, and it seems I need to be. Always ready.

I don't really have too many friends at school. Everyone seems to get along with me, but I don't fit in to any of the groups that have formed and neatly split the year group into six cliques. Over recent months, Daniel and I have become good friends mainly because we've each needed someone. He is kind of out of control and I feel like there is a chance that things are going to turn bad for us at any point. We are a strange looking pair. The short and stout alongside the long and thin.

We snuck down to the creek during interval. We had a couple of smokes and split the contents of his hip flask. Daniel drank heaps more than me. How he was meant to play the trumpet in that state was beyond me. He stands on a box to be seen when he plays a solo. If he'd had one in the second half, he probably would have fallen off. When we were on our way back, he pulled out a spray can and started graffitiing a wall. The prospect of him being caught were high but he didn't care. He seemed to be in a constant drive to get caught, to seek attention in negative ways. He never appears to pay a price for anything, and it seemed like his attitude was designed as a dare to the powers that be.

'They try to punish me, and I will play the persecuted, victimised, disabled child,' he'd say leaving me in no doubt the dangers in being too involved with him. All it required was for me to be guilty of the same thing and I would be penalised in any way seen fit. I wasn't smart enough to stop hanging around with him, but the spray can was never going to be in my hand.

Daniel may get me in trouble in time, but Mr. Harris, or Stuart as he insists on me calling him, is a much bigger problem.

I don't know how to explain it. Some men are into other men rather than women. Well, Stuart never seemed like that sort of guy. Turns out, he kind of is, but rather than other men, he likes much younger males. Boys. And I seem to be the boy he wants to be with, or at least one of them.

Last night at the end of the concert we got into his car and took the long drive across town to his house. Plenty of the other teachers saw him taking me home, so it obviously is normal enough to have this sort of interaction between teachers and their former students. That's the very thing that has me feeling so uncertain about all this, but I still can't help but feel it isn't right. I guess if it was just dropping me home it wouldn't be an issue, but it's the awkward strangeness from the moments we are back at his place that don't seem right.

I know there is more than one bedroom at his house so it would have been no problem for me to sleep in the spare room. Except, he doesn't want me sleeping in a separate room. He wants to be sleeping with me. This clearly isn't just a question of convenience. This must be the way he wants it.

Like he has done every other time I have been there, he's put sheets down on the floor in front of the television in the living room. The first time I was here that seemed to make sense, but last night there was no reason for it. It was late when we had got home, and it wasn't like we were going to stay up watching anything for too long. I guess I already knew what was going on enough to know that it had nothing to do with the television.

Every contact I have had with him had seen him take things a small step further. Last time he had touched me, front and back but while we were both pretending to be asleep. Was he going to avoid the sleep pretence and make me really face it? Was I going to have to be exposed to his dick this time and if so, how? I'd learnt enough since I was last here to know what sort of things someone like that can want. I can't fucking do that. I'm also too scared of him to say no. What if he does force any of those things on me?

When we were in the car, I had a vision of Edward O'Connor. I saw him looking through the windscreen and then his eyes close as the car crashed. I thought in that moment that the best possible thing would be for Stuart to crash the car and kill us. Death was less scary than what he may put me through, for at least it was quick, it was final and there would be no need to keep recounting the experience over and again. The same could not be said for what he was planning.

It didn't happen. We made it back to his house safely. Needless to say, I was petrified from the moment we walked in the door.

As much as I was too afraid to say anything to anyone, I knew that he had certain fears as well. He isn't allowed to do this with someone my age. Even if the school thinks it is alright to for teachers to have sleepovers with students, I'm certain they're not allowed to have sex with them. He may well think I'm too scared to say anything about him, but he has a bit of fear that if he goes too far too fast that I just might and then he'll be in trouble. Within my deepest fear, the one thing that might help save me is his own fear.

I felt incredibly tired when I first laid down, but that was irrelevant. There was no way I would be sleeping given the fears of what he would do. I kind of wished I could. Imagine how good it would be to be able to sleep through it all. Surely anything he would do wouldn't matter if I didn't know about it. I wasn't going to find out though, as I laid there allowing my eyes to close but with mind on the highest level of alert.

It seemed to take less time than previously before his body closed in on mine. I could feel his hardness pressed against me, but his pyjama pants were still on. His arm was wrapped tightly around me, his hand moving between my chest and stomach. I focused on breathing loudly, thinking I was making it sound like I was asleep and lightly snoring. It may have been obvious to him that I wasn't, but I was desperately trying to avoid any form of confrontation. He lightly pulled on my t-shirt, untucking it from my pyjama pants and then left his hand on my bare skin.

I wasn't completely certain he was awake. His movements were so slow and silent, that it was possible he was asleep, and all of his turning and touching was just incidental. Sometimes his hand moved, always down, but it seemed more like the fall of a relaxed limb than a selective movement. I became more uncomfortable each time, as the hand always seemed to end up in the worst possible spot. I tried to roll over to ensure his hand was no longer in the same spot, but it proved to be of little use. He was not going to stop doing what he wanted. I'm sure he had everything planned and nothing I did was going to change it other than direct confrontation. In my head, I already had ruled this out. Confrontation would make him angry. Making him angry would be the most dangerous action. I was a prisoner in his house. Raising the stakes was as dangerous as offering myself completely. My only option was to continue as I was doing and accepting whatever happened.

I'm too embarrassed to explain the night. It became more obvious he was pretending to be asleep. I pretended to be asleep. When there was a mess, I got up ready to pretend that I'd had a funny dream if he asked me. I hate that such a thing happened because if people ever knew that detail, they would think that I liked it. Nothing could be further from the truth. I was scared and I couldn't control how my body reacted. He is the only person who has ever touched me that way and I my body just took over.

When I went back to the makeshift bed, he pretended to stir and asked if everything was alright. I said yes and lay on the outside edge of the sheets. He stayed his distance, but after enough time he decided I would be asleep again, and he moved right back against me.

There were other things I don't want to think about. He didn't do as much as I feared but I guess in his head this is step 10 of 20. He will be planning to keep bringing me back here. Every time going a step further until he has done every sick thing he wants to do with me.

I wonder if all of this is what he did with David Wallace? I wonder if he has done the same with heaps of other boys. Maybe when he leaves it a long time between invitations it is because he has a different boy lined up in each of the other weeks. He probably has a journal where he keeps track of where he is up to with each boy. We are all just toys for him to play with. Shit. I'm even dumber than I thought.

He commented that I seemed a bit quiet this morning and told him that I had a bit of a headache. I wasn't sure whether it was wise or not, but I said that I slept a bit funny because I had some weird dreams. He didn't say too much but had a bit of a smirk on his face before saying he was sorry to hear about the headache.

'Weird dreams aren't always bad though,' he said without elaborating any further. There was so much awkwardness. I knew that he knew what I had meant. We both found it safer to avoid the truth being open. He got me breakfast and then said he'd drop me home straight after I had my shower.

When I got in the shower, I spent most of the time looking around the room wondering if there was a hole in the wall or a video camera set up somewhere. Knowing how much he liked to touch me, I started thinking that he probably would like to see me naked. Maybe that's why he had Mr. Mooney over last time, so they could look at me together. Better than having them touching me I guess, but I still don't think it should happen. Like previously I was very quickly out of the shower and covered up, keen to ensure that if id missed his vantage point he was going to have as little opportunity as possible.

'That was quick,' he commented, almost as if to reprimand me for compromising his pleasure.

I didn't know how to respond so just kept walking back to the kitchen table without saying anything at first before commenting again on my headache. He didn't give me anything for it, but within a few minutes we were on the road back to my place.

I don't care how difficult it is, I am not going to allow this to happen again. It scares me to think of where this will end up. However much I want to be accepted, it's not by him. Fitting in nowhere is much better than fitting in somewhere like this. I don't care what excuses it takes, when he asks, I will say no. That might feel uncomfortable, but a hell of a lot less uncomfortable than I feel when I am with him.

'They try to punish me, and I will play the persecuted, victimised, disabled child.' Daniel's words last night rang in my ears. He didn't care about getting caught doing anything

wrong, as he'd avoid punishment by what he would say to the authorities who were afraid to test him. Did Stuart have a similar set of words he'd use on the school authorities? On the police? He seemed equally as unconcerned about getting caught doing anything wrong. He didn't hide my presence from Mr. Mooney. He didn't hide taking me home from the school last night. He gave as little attempt to secrecy as Daniel did.

When he dropped me home, he said he'd call me soon and we'd arrange another catch up then. I nodded my head as I got out the door, but internally I was adamant that there would be no next time. He may have the authorities within the school protecting him, and allowing him to do what he wants, but that doesn't mean I have to let them. So what if they seek to punish me? I don't care what the consequences he or the school threaten, I will not allow this to happen again. I will not be his toy. I don't care if it's what I deserve. I am never going to be alone with him again.

CHAPTER 19

8.34AM

A few weeks after the concert, Stuart contacted me again. He was desperate to see me in the next couple of weeks, as he was being transferred to Brisbane for a teacher exchange. Teacher exchange? This had been very unexpected. Had the consequences of David's suicide led to this? Had another one of his other victims said something that had led the school to act? Perhaps the school had panicked about the situation and tried to get him out of there. They probably didn't care about protecting him but wanted to protect their reputation and any legal liability they would face. While I found excuses to be unavailable to see him in the next couple of weeks, Stuart knew that my mother lived in Brisbane, and I visited regularly in school holidays. He told me I should come and see him when I was next there.

I never saw him again.

I wanted to see him, but on my terms. I don't know what those terms would be. At times I thought a courtroom, so I could see him brought to justice, yet that meant facing my own shame.

At times I wanted to shoot him, stab him, do anything to inflict physical pain on him as vengeance for the torment he caused me. I've never been violent enough to throw a punch in my life, so for all the hate I feel, I know I couldn't see this through. Maybe, just maybe, I could spit on him. What would it achieve? Really, the result of never seeing him again was the best one yet it never gave me closure.

I've always believed that the best revenge is living well. Sadly, on that score, I have failed to get my revenge. I haven't lived well. I still bear the scars he caused. I've had therapy, I've had medication and at times I have felt like I have fully overcome the traumas. Thinking I've completely moved on, the past then climbs right back into the present. Sometimes news stories about paedophiles trigger the memories. Sometimes they came from nowhere.

Every person has opinions that are formed based on their experiences in life. So many people have opinions on this topic that come from ideals they have. Sometimes they are formed from hearing the experiences of others, but most of those opinions are full of shit. Nobody experienced exactly what I did. Yes, millions of people in this world have experienced worse, but nobody's experience is identical. Nobody can therefore tell me what I should feel. There is no should, just what is. I feel what I feel based on what I experienced.

I became a target for him because of my nature, and that was the result of every experience in my life before that time. Once he began to prey on me, and once I had been his victim, those experiences shaped every moment of my life that followed. Anxieties, insecurities, inability to trust, sexual dysfunction, depression, suicidal ideation all became part of life. I did not choose these reactions.

In some ways paedophiles are like artists. They have the capacity to see things in a way others don't, identifying the most suitable subjects to work on. They hone their craft with each piece, identifying the strengths and weaknesses of their work and how they can develop their style for a result they will consider superior. Each new child is like a new canvas as they begin their quest. Where they differ is the direct opposite result of their work. A canvas is enriched by the vision of an artist while a child is destroyed when they are the target. An artist's work is for the appreciation of others whereas a paedophiles work destroys others, all for their own sick self-satisfaction. I hate that I exist in the portfolio within his mind. He might not have photos, but he has his memories. He can have wanked a thousand times at the thought of the child I was.

Last year he was jailed for offences against another child. It was good news to hear that he had received some form of justice. It wasn't justice for me, but it was a degree of justice for him. It pleases me that the public record shows that this man is a paedophile, he is a predator, he betrays the trust of his victims and their families. I don't need to be recognised as a victim for those facts to be certain. Whoever he has done this to, his monstrous nature cannot be questioned. I read quite a bit about the case and while the circumstances were different, there was a similar pattern to the grooming process. His molestation of that child predated him knowing me by more than eight years, so he had clearly built a methodology with time.

Through the time that this case was in the media the impact on me was traumatic. While the result was what I wanted, it was a constant reminder of all that had happened. Every ride to work was playing out the memories. If only I hadn't been so scared and was able to speak out. If only others had protected me. If only other victims had spoken out sooner, surely he would have been stopped before. I probably suffered the consequences of the molestation more last year than I had in the previous twenty years. It certainly wasn't justice for me however appreciative I was of the verdict.

His justice doesn't mean he can't still haunt my thoughts. I still fantasise at the thought of having the word paedophile painfully tattooed across his forehead. That alone would probably be enough to make me feel better. Maybe it wouldn't. He might live another ten or twenty years, so he will only have ten to twenty years of a ruined life from this, whether in jail or tortured or anything else. His impact on me has already lasted thirty-five years and the thirty-fifth year has been no less significant than when it happened. I have every reason to believe he'll always be there. I've had counselling, I've learnt, I've grown, and I feel I'm as adjusted as I ever can be. We are all the product of every experience we have ever had. I can't eliminate an experience from the past. This is forever part of me. He is forever part of me. He is the reminder of evil.

There have been many studies that have shown that a sizable proportion of paedophiles were victims themselves in their own upbringing. Is this what made Stuart the monster he is? Maybe, but it isn't even a semblance of a justification. Being the victim of something shouldn't normalise it but rather it should scream at you the evil of its nature. For me, there is no punishment too great for paedophiles. That's a popular enough view with the average person, but I feel so much more resolute than the average person on this topic. I lived it and continue to see flashbacks to this day. His face will never completely disappear from my memory. I would rather be dead than to ever ruin a child in that way. Maybe somewhere within him is guilt for the lives he ruined, but that doesn't change anything. He calmly and calculatedly chose his path. If someone made him what he was, he still knew enough about that to make his choice. He chose evil. Given the chance, I'd choose his death.

Harris left me a shadow of the person I'd been. I could act the role of Anthony and I could do it well enough that people accepted what they wanted to see. The truth was dark because that's what life had become. It felt like life was moving in one direction. Who would be digging the hole for me next was a mystery, yet it seemed certain that the light was going to continue fading with time.

A few minutes ago, I was nearly knocked over and seriously injured. In this moment, I wish I had been. Once again, I face the reality that I carry a life sentence as the victim, while he as the perpetrator will never get what he deserves.

The lights change and I must make an instant decision whether to stop or go. I stop. I need my head clearer.

CHAPTER 20

8.36AM

Many of the heavy trucks from interstate come down Glen Osmond Road, and every morning at least a couple will pass me. For as long as I can remember, the temptation of turning my handlebars and moving in front of them has never been far from my mind. I always fear my timing wouldn't be good enough to finalise things and I'd survive with permanent handicaps. I'm too weak to endure that. My desires are only for the ultimate result. I think it's highly disturbing that the most positive thoughts I have are about death, yet sadly that's what life has become.

Plotting to get myself killed so soon after I slammed on brakes to avoid that fate seems ironic. Or is it ironic? Does anyone really want to endure the pain of life if they can find an easy escape? I don't think I understand people enough to make that call anymore.

Thinking about the car accident and then the abuse, I tend to arrive at this mindset. It doesn't need to be those events that lead me here, though usually they're the starting point even if there are indirect turns along the way.

I was an awkward teen. Right or wrong, my recollection of childhood is that I was an average kid. Didn't stand out in any way. As I moved through my teens, it seemed like I became two different people. One who everyone saw as happy, outgoing, and friendly while the other was a mix of angst and hatred and lay buried within. It was the latter that felt real, but I was determined to keep him hidden from the world. The conflict between the two came in certain uncomfortable situations where I just couldn't silence the boy within.

Lust is at the forefront of almost every boy's experience of being a teen. While this was somewhat true for me as well, the experiences I'd had meant the transition from fantasy to reality carried many additional complications. I wanted to hit the erase button on my past and begin again with a girl who shared my nerves and my excitement. Life doesn't offer a rewind option, so the anxieties proved to be permanent fixtures.

Jacqui, Melissa, Rachel, and Kate all took turns in being the object of my attention and affection. All of them disappeared from my life as quickly as they appeared. When Michelle came along things were different. I didn't initially feel any great attraction to her, and that was probably perfect. I got to know her without all my thinking being done in my pants. She really liked me, far more than I did her. I got along well with her, she made me laugh, and I enjoyed spending time with her. It was like being with one of the boys. It meant, for the first time, I didn't have the normal fears that plagued my interaction with girls. One night with a couple of drinks into us, we kissed. My feelings seemed to change in an instant. Now, I knew she really was a girl. I never had to question or contemplate what I wanted from that moment despite the fact she was so completely opposite to what I had generally looked for.

I always loved femininity, and that certainly was not Michelle. She had short hair that looked like a boys cut. She never wore skirts or dresses and was always most comfortable in a t-shirt and track pants or jeans. She loved sport which was one of the major foundations of our blossoming relationship. We also had similar taste in music and movies. More than anything, we genuinely understood and appreciated each other's sarcastic sense of humour. We fed off each other and spent so much time laughing, often at the most inappropriate times and places.

She was as awkward as me in many ways. There was an undoubted upside and downside to this. It held us back at times, knowing that we could each rely on the other to say no whenever anything confronting arose. We loved that, but of course that was the principle of taking the easy option. We facilitated easy options for each other. Incredibly comfortable as it was, it didn't serve us best.

Though she had very much been the instigator of the relationship, she was very apprehensive about anything physical. A boy at that age always has his foot on the accelerator, yet my experiences had left me very apprehensive about anything sexual. I was incredibly patient, but still Michelle frustrated me. We would lie on my bed or hers, our parents probably convinced we were rooting like rabbits, yet we'd merely be watching a movie or a sporting event on TV. At the appropriate times we'd kiss, we'd touch, but one step too far and she would push back. My experiences meant that the first sign of hesitancy from her and I would retreat at lightning pace, but it didn't stop me feeling disappointed and a little insecure.

While the relationship took a long time to reach the point I wanted, I never contemplated moving on from it because so much was great. She was as messed up as me and I never knew why. She never knew why I was, because as close as we were I couldn't share my scars. I often wondered, and still do, if she had experienced something similar in her younger years. She never seemed able to let go. Even as time passed, sex remained the one time when we felt awkward together. Before sex was a little uncomfortable, during sex was very awkward and after sex was a nightmare. All the compatibility that defined every conversation would fly out the window until we were both dressed and had another completely unrelated topic arise for us. I wish I had been able to talk to her about what I'd been through. Maybe, it would have served as an opportunity for her to do the same. Maybe both of us would have reached a whole new point in moving forward, by knowing we could do it safely together.

At that point of life, the sum of my experiences had taught me that sex had a couple of ways it could work. It could be a power game that a predator uses to squeeze the life out of a victim. Equally, it could be an awkward experience. In this case, you have immense physical pleasure with a girl who seems to want to be anywhere else and wants it to be over as quickly as possible. Luckily for her, 'as quick as possible' was my specialty at this age. Less fortunate for us both was the strong variance between when I was ready again and when she was. For me 10 times a week sounded a good starting point, despite our lack of opportunities. Michelle seemed to think that once a year would be ideal.

Time was destined to change our relationship one way or another. She was nine months younger than me. I had known her since I was fifteen, we had technically been a couple since I was sixteen and first slept together when I was seventeen. When it changed, why it changed and how it changed is something I've never really reconciled. I think I really noticed the change just after her seventeenth birthday. Jokes began falling flat. The agreement that we would always find in what movie to watch now disappeared. It wasn't genre related, but almost an act of spite that meant whatever I suggested was not appealing to her. Even if I knew it was a favourite film of hers, she'd be against it purely on my suggestion. To be fair the same would happen in reverse, so it wasn't that one of us was acting alone in this way.

We were both so non-confrontational in nature that we never fought or argued. We never talked about what was wrong. We rarely made plans, I would just turn up at her house or she'd come to mine. We were both studying at the same campus and whenever we weren't in class, we were together. but that started changing, as she started going home as soon as her classes were finished. She stopped coming to my place and I stopped going to hers. She would have justified her actions based on mine, and I did the same thing. When we saw each other, we would still greet each other with a kiss on the cheek, but spending time together became more laboured.

Eventually I told her that I wanted her to meet someone else. She reacted badly as she felt I was making it out as her fault. She suggested that by her meeting someone else, I would avoid having to take any action. I explained that I was sure we both weren't enjoying spending time together and I didn't know why it was that way. I told her that I didn't blame her at all. I merely wanted both of us to enjoy our lives more and that would only happen if we were ready to move forward which I couldn't see happening without some sort of trigger point.

'You mean *you* want to see someone else,' her words still clear to me a quarter of a century later. She was right though, I did. Not anyone in particular, but I felt stuck. It was like I was obligated to stay faithful to Michelle despite not being in a genuine relationship with her. Part of what I'd become was someone who couldn't be the bad guy, so it felt like my only escape was for her to force it.

'I don't want to meet someone else, but yeah I am sick of this,' she admitted. 'You don't have any idea how much you've changed, and I just don't enjoy our time together. I don't hate you. I miss who you were, but I know you're not him anymore.'

'So, you think it is *me* who has changed? Not you? *I* am the cause?'

'No, I believe that we have,' she said. 'We're humans, we do, constantly. Relationships thrive when you change in similar ways, move in the same direction. You and I haven't. When I say that you're not the same person anymore, it is about not being the same relative to me. It is the changes in me as much as those in you that has done that. Not every issue has to be a case where someone's right and someone's wrong. This is what it is. No blame.'

I still blamed her. I don't know if it is an indicator of the way my mind works, but the ending of the relationship that wasn't, had me an inconsolable mess for a long time. Michelle had been so perfect, not that I realised this at any point until we had broken up. I didn't understand what she meant about me changing. I don't think I changed at all. She changed. She stopped laughing at my jokes. I stopped laughing with her because she stopped being funny. Everything I could see highlighted how it was her alone who had changed. What was different about me? Either way, why did I care? I had wanted this uncomfortable situation to end. When it did, I was a depressed mess who felt like I had sabotaged a wonderful relationship. I felt like I'd been thrown out like trash and the only person who had ever been interested in the trash that others neglected was that evil prick, Harris. Is that what I'm good for?

Fuck, it isn't healthy to think this way riding down such a busy road. Again, my way is blocked by a gutter driver, but I'm conscious not to go around the vehicle as I see that traffic is just about to move again.

Through the rest of my time at university, I saw Michelle no more than four or five times as I did all I could to dodge her. I had moved on, but nothing had ever seemed as right as it had been with her. I still was upset and I didn't want her to see the impact she'd had. Equally I wouldn't have wanted to see her in any way that would leave me feeling guilty. She was largely a loner the whole time I'd known her, and every time I saw her it was walking between buildings on her own. No sign of moving on, she was the same Michelle I'd always known. Still the same awkward girl who seemed to have found no way of moving forward with any sort of positivity. Did I miss something along the way? Could a different approach have avoided things ending like this? In the scheme of where life went, it's hard to imagine that she really was *the one*. Is there even such a thing as *the one*? Are the happiest couples those who have found their one perfect person, or are they more skilled at making things perfect?

It was probably five years later when I next saw her. I was between relationships, and we ran into each other at a mutual friend's wedding. We spent most of the evening laughing like we did at seventeen. I couldn't help but wonder again where it all went wrong, as we connected so perfectly. She drove me home and I invited her in. We had a coffee and continued the banter. I thought for a fleeting moment that this may have been a new beginning. Maybe she did too, but neither of us was quite able to seize the moment. We thanked each other for the night, wished each other well and said we would see each other again soon. More than twenty years later, and I have never seen her again. I have no idea where she is and what has become of her life. So many people disappear from our lives despite having had enormous impacts at a point in time. She'll surely never know about today. I wouldn't know that she hasn't already lived her version of it.

90% of my memories of Michelle are great, yet being a Monday morning, I seem to have got way too caught up in the other 10%.

The honk of a car horn brings me back to the present. It wasn't aimed at me, but a car trying to change lanes and nearly swiping the side mirror of someone else. Typically, it is a Suzuki, like Michelle was driving in that last moment I ever saw her.

For all the angst, I think back at how other relationships ended for me and really this wasn't so bad. After Michelle I met Renee, and while I had a great few months with her, I found out she was having an even greater few months. Not only with me, but with at least three other guys. That still wasn't enough for me to end it, but the obvious jealousy I showed led to her breaking up with me. Again, I was uncontrollably distraught, but I was far less successful in avoiding her for any time. It was only a week later before I came face to face with her.

CHAPTER 21

SATURDAY OCTOBER 8, 1993

'I don't want to be there if she is,' I told Griffin.

'And do what instead?' he asked.

Last weekend Renee dumped me. I know people think I'm overreacting to it, but feelings aren't dictated by choice. I seem to be getting more sensitive to rejection and disappointment as time goes by. Maybe that's the impact from the bad things that have happened in my life. I know terrible things happen to everyone, but maybe I'm just worse at dealing with it.

Griffin eventually talked me into it. Sean would be there, but he and Nikki would probably be too preoccupied with each other for me to even see them. Really, the main reason for going was Renee. The person I least wanted to see was strangely enough also the one person I most wanted to see. I don't know why, but I wanted her to see that I was hurt. I didn't expect she'd feel guilty, though maybe my presence just may ever so slightly diminish her enjoyment of the evening. If I can't feel good, then the best I can hope for is making someone I don't like to feel bad. No wonder my father is adamant I'm not growing up.

Nikki and Renee are best friends. When I started going out with Renee, the four of us started spending a lot of time together. Now as I arrived at Brendan's house, the new dynamic was clear and on display. We were like the cast of a soap opera, only my character had seen a new actor come into play my role. I looked across the room and saw the new guy, Kane. Wanker more like it. I didn't like him. I wasn't the confrontational type, so I would not be making any issues. Then again, I wasn't going to be doing much else there beyond drinking until I forgot what the problem was in the first place.

Nikki lived next door to Brendan, which was how the range of connections originated. Brendan and I used to get lifts to and from school together, and from that Griffin and Sean joined us in becoming closer when we finished high school. We all ended up interacting with a group of Nikki's friends. Being a couple of years younger, they were still at the local public school. While it was us guys and those girls, all was good. The same did not apply to Kane coming into the mix.

'He's a dickhead,' Sean told me, 'I'm stuck with him. So long as he's with Renee, he's gonna be around the place too much for my liking. You can at least stay away from him. Nikki won't give me that option.'

There weren't many people at Brendan's, so avoiding anyone in particular was going to be impossible. Renee couldn't dodge me for long, but it was just a quick hello before disappearing as far away as she could get.

A couple of the girls had taken command of the stereo at one stage and had been playing music that my ears didn't appreciate. Once the CD they had on finished and I couldn't see them, I flicked it over to the radio for what I thought would be something more neutral. It wasn't going to suit everyone, but as Joy Division's 'Love Will Tear Us Apart,' began on the radio, I briefly got my way.

I walked back to the kitchen to grab a beer, only seconds later to hear Ian Curtis's baritone voice replaced by some sort of crap that probably emanated from a band at the local school. I stormed back in to flick the switch back to the radio and saw that it was Renee who'd switched it over.

'Just this one song, ok' I said, turning the radio back on.

I walked back to my beer, and she did the same thing.

'Why not just *my* one song' she said.

'You've got the disc, mines on the radio. Once that ends, you've got all night.' For the third time I flicked the switch. Renee was enjoying the game too much though. Rather than flick it back to the disc, she disconnected the power, so everyone lost. She looked at me and laughed.

'You can't win,' she told me.

I walked back out to the kitchen, furious. I noticed a knife sitting on the bench and without hesitation I picked it up. I marched back to the living room yelling out her name with the blade in the air. She had reconnected the power and put the CD back on.

'Put the radio back on' I yelled as I moved towards her. She immediately moved back, instinct dictating her moves at the sight of danger. Before I got any closer, Brendan had leapt in like a superhero, grabbing me from behind, taking complete control of my arms and rendering the knife useless.

'Na,' Renee laughed, 'I think we're done.'

I was fighting against Brendan, but very half-heartedly. He was substantially bigger than me so there was little I would have been able to achieve, but I didn't want to look so clearly defeated in front of her.

Through the whole incident, Kane had been outside smoking weed. He came in around this point and asked what the noise had been about. Renee told him that we'd just had an argument about music but nothing more. Most people wouldn't have retained such composure, but it was clear that she did because she had a better idea of what was going on than anyone else.

'What the fuck were you thinking,' Brendan said as he got me outside.

'Thanks man, I owe you,' I said.

'What?'

'You authenticated my performance. You know I'm completely incapable of hurting anyone. I wanted to scare her. She deserved that. More, really. Didn't work much. She remained relaxed the whole time cos she knew I wouldn't touch her. The only time she did look nervous was after you'd grabbed me, and I genuinely looked to be fighting against you to get to her. For a moment she wondered. *Could he actually do something like that?*'

'What would you have done if Brendan did nothing?' Griffin asked, having also been nervous but curious of just how far I would have gone.

'I would run towards her with the knife then offered it to her and see if she wanted to stab me in the heart. She was just about doing as much in every other action she ever took towards me.'

I didn't really want to stay but I didn't have many other options. I stayed and before too long crossed paths with Renee again.

'Sorry,' she said. Most people would have thought that it was me that should be offering the apology, but Renee understood the situation. She knew that the knife was a performance, not a threat and that the stereo didn't matter, it was just a test of wills. I'm not sure she ever really wanted to be with me. Looking back, I think she probably just saw me as a way of strengthening her friendship with Nikki whose focus was now Sean. Without saying anything, I think that was what she was apologising for.

'Me too. About earlier. You knew I wouldn't ever have done anything, right?'

'Yeah. But still, don't make a habit of it. Other people mightn't get it.'

I nodded sheepishly, and we moved off. I was ready to go home. All I wanted was some sort of acknowledgement on her part that she'd treated me badly. With that received, my night had peaked and the idea of being around others wasn't appealing. I let Griffin know I was going and quietly disappeared.

'You alright?' Griffin wasn't one to wear his heart on his sleeve, but I never had a friend who was more willing to do anything for me. I told him to stay at the party and I'd see him the next day.

It's only a ten-minute walk home from Brendan's. It is quiet and it is cold, so I walk briskly. Was this another example of running away when it's difficult? I felt like turning up tonight was going completely against my normal approach, but it wasn't really. I only turned up to get attention, not to confront an issue. When I confronted an issue, I still only did it in a way that couldn't have a legitimate consequence. Maybe I'm just learning how to make it appear I'm evolving, when I'm just relying on a security blanket.

Renee and I had been convenient for each other and that is what led to us ever going out together. Through our time, we never seemed suited, but in that last conversation it seemed like she understood me more than anyone else does. Now that it's over, for the first time I can see how it could have been something amazing.

Is it only when someone leaves or abandons me that I genuinely want them? It was like that with Michelle as well, but also with family and friends. They all seemed to be standing in my way until they were gone. Vulnerability and rejection are what Harris picked up on his radar and drew him to me. Ever since, my reactions to rejection have become progressively worse.

Maybe I need to be on my own. Nobody can leave you if nobody is with you to begin.

CHAPTER 22

8.37AM

I'm stopped at the lights near the local primary school. Across the road is the sign for Jenny's. Thankfully, the difficulty of getting across such a busy road at this time of the day is enough to stop me. Their pastries are amazing but remain an occasional indulgence. There is no way I could afford a stop in their shop to become a routine part of my work day. They close before I pass on the way home which is when I would be most vulnerable to the temptation. I would have made an excuse today if only time had allowed it.

It has always been nothing more than an occasional weekend treat, but that means that it retains the ultimate level of appreciation. My ex-wife Cleo always used to tell me that anything you experience often enough will always be less appreciated than a rare treat. Beer, sex, travel, chocolate.

'Too often and you'll appreciate it less,' she said.

'Well, we can have sex once a year and I will feel amazing once. Or we can have sex once a night and I will feel almost as amazing 365 times. I think I'll go with less appreciation more often, thanks.'

Not that she was wrong in theory, but in practice, it is hard to say no to having more of the things you love.

While pastries usually occupy my mind when I look at Jenny's, today I'm focused more on the name Jenny than the bakery. Jenny Duggan worked in my office in 2005. She was about my age, attractive and she initially seemed like everything I was looking for. Soon after I found out she was in a relationship, and I would be wasting my time. I still got along really well with her and we often spent lunchtimes together.

Jenny invited me to her engagement party which I really didn't want to go to. I was sure that I'd know hardly anyone there. Environments with a lot of people I don't know are always uncomfortable, but I liked Jenny enough that I wanted to avoid lying to her. I was well aware that she'd know I was lying if I did come up with some flimsy excuse for not going.

Luckily I did turn up, as that was the night I met Cleo. She also worked in our building, in an area where Jenny had previously worked. I had recognised her from the lifts, but being on a different floor, never had the opportunity of an ice-breaker. We started talking at the party and pretty much never stopped. We flowed the way that Michelle and I had years earlier, yet there was so much more to Cleo. I thought that she was out of my league and accepted that it wouldn't last, but I should just enjoy it for what it was. Easier said than done for an irrational mind, but one way or another it seemed to pay off. We seemed to move through each phase of our relationship quickly and painlessly. I was probably insecure enough in myself, that I was willing ignore the little negatives I would see from time to time. I shouldn't say negatives; incompatibilities would be far more suitable. No doubt there were at least as many negatives of mine that she was overlooking. She was a little obsessive compulsive which aggravated me, but I was happy enough with the overall relationship to allow myself to wallow too much in any negatives.

'Anthony and Cleopatra,' Dad said after meeting her.

'Um, you know how that ended, right?'

Never the history student, he didn't, but after a brief explanation it was safe that he'd never say it again. Which is not to say we didn't hear that line from other people at times going forward.

The great challenge for me came when Cleo decided she needed to move back to her original home of the Gold Coast. It wasn't her responsibility to be close to her parents and grandparents, yet she felt the need. Multiple family members had endured significant health issues and she felt that she really should be close by them. She wanted me to come and start life with her up there. Living in Adelaide had made her feel isolated from her family and the combination of her sister just having given birth to a baby boy and her father having been diagnosed with cancer meant she felt desperate to return. The fact that this was likely to leave me as the isolated one didn't seem to register to her. The fact that I had my mother reasonably close in suburban Brisbane, reduced the significance of this. The thought of moving closer to my mother was appealing, though it would mean leaving my father here with no other family. Admittedly there wasn't much else I would be leaving behind in Adelaide other than heartache and bad memories. It wasn't an easy choice.

As a child I had run away to the Gold Coast. Now I would be running towards it. All I could have run away from was the relationship, and that would have meant staying in Adelaide. It felt safer, but I knew that so-called safety was destructive for me. I needed to stop running away. I joined her.

It was less than a year from us meeting, and we were starting a new life together on Chevron Island at Surfers Paradise. Less than a year later we were engaged, and we were married days after my 34th birthday. Three days before our first wedding anniversary we welcomed our first child into the world.

Olivia.

When Cleo came into my life everything seemed like a slightly better version of what had come before. With each step we had taken together, life had a pleasant extra element, but nothing that seemed brand new or life altering. The day Olivia was born, life truly altered. It wasn't just in a practical sense but emotionally. I felt a love that was completely different. Not only did we create a life that was ready to define me in every way, but I felt an attachment to Cleo that was infinitely more powerful than it had been at any previous stage of our relationship. Saying forever in a church had seemed relatively meaningless at the time, but now my reflection on that day was even less significant again. Olivia was the proof that Cleo and I were destined forever.

For nearly four months I felt life had a level of meaning that I'd always searched for. Olivia was perfection and every aspect of life was worthwhile as I did everything to make her life as perfect as she was. Cleo at times seemed to be part of this utopia, though I sense that she hid some of her feelings from me. I don't know so much that she was experiencing post-natal depression, but I suspect that after I had returned to work and she became the 24-hour a day parent, that she yearned for moments of escape. Olivia was as easy as a baby can be, but even the simplest infant requires an enormous amount. The drain naturally had some level of impact on Cleo.

While Cleo and I seemed to have lost something from our earlier days, it was like losing a cent and finding a dollar. Olivia had brought everything we wanted into our lives. Appreciating all you have in life is often as the most dangerous thing you can do. Nothing, however simple, remains guaranteed.

Dammit, if only Jenny's had put donuts into my head instead of Jenny Duggan, I wouldn't have put myself through all this right now. The temptation to turn around and get a donut runs through my head but just as quickly I think about my 9am meeting and proceed onwards.

CHAPTER 23

MONDAY NOVEMBER 28, 2011

There have been times when I had believed I knew the worst that life can be. I now understand how wrong I had been. Today I have experienced a moment that can never be surpassed. No hell could be filled with anything that would destroy a person like this.

I say today, but it was actually last night. I haven't slept, so yesterday and today serve as one for me and I don't know how long it will be before I sleep. I don't know if I ever will sleep properly again.

Olivia always sleeps so well. We never have the kind of drama so many parents consider normal when it comes to putting her down. We have no real roster, but whichever one of us puts her to bed, the other is in moments later to make sure we get our last cuddle of the evening and to feel that reassurance and comfort of seeing her so peaceful.

Olivia's cot is still in our bedroom. We both feel like she is ready to move into her own room, yet we share the view that it is reassuring having her close. The soundness of her sleep means there is little for us to gain by moving her, so we had agreed that we didn't need to put too much consideration into it until she's closer to twelve months. It is one of the few things we've had ease in discussing and agreeing to.

I'd been late leaving work this afternoon and was home only briefly before Cleo put her to bed. As always, I was in soon after, but didn't disturb her seeing how soundly she was sleeping. Comfortable, peaceful, and healthy.

I hadn't had dinner at this stage, and Cleo had put in the microwave to get it ready for me. I wanted us to talk. I knew she was struggling and that was having an impact on me too. Although we talked there proved to be little point. We are a strange combination. In any characteristic you can think of we are either opposite or identical, with no middle ground. We seem to be equally as unable or unwilling to openly discuss issues, yet our views on any issue couldn't be more different. Talking tonight seemed to get us as far as the first sign of seeing things differently before we returned to the security of silence.

Around about 10pm Cleo told me she was going to bed. An incidental piece of information such was the emotional distance between us, but relevant in that she would be checking on Olivia and saving me the need. In earlier times we'd be checking her constantly, but this had become less and less relevant for our own peace of mind more than for any need of Olivia's.

As I logged on to the home computer to check my emails, I heard a scream like nothing ever before. I sprinted from the back of the house to the source of the scream in the bedroom. With no prior reason to know what may have happened, perhaps it was merely my history of pessimism and bad results that had me already knowing what I was going to find.

Cleo was simultaneously crying and screaming incoherently while holding Olivia as I entered the room.

'She's blue, she's not breathing, she's gone.' Cleo released another blood curdling scream as I grabbed my baby girl from my wife. I shook her, trying anything I could to get a response. To make something, anything happen. I soon made a similar scream to what Cleo had previously done. I sank to my knees, in tears.

'There has to be a way,' I cried as I passed her lifeless body back to Cleo. I called the ambulance immediately refusing to believe it was too late. It may have been obvious, but accepting it was impossible. By the time I'd got the details out of what and where, I was again incoherent, the sound of my screams and tears as I began to understand the futility of the call. My little girl was gone. There would be nothing that could be done.

Time seemed to stand still. It seemed like the paramedics were with us before I'd even finished on the phone. Neighbours had heard the screams and were out the front when the ambulances turned up. I'm sure they spoke to me, offering any assistance they could provide, but words didn't sink in. I was living a nightmare. All too often people use this word as a metaphor for a bad experience, but this was like the true nightmare of our sleep, with no coherence between the disturbing, gruesome images before us. Even as I looked at others, all I could see was Olivia, either blue, or screaming. I kept screaming too.

Moments behind the paramedics were the police. Shit, as though the grief and tragedy isn't overpowering enough, the reality is this is a sudden death. They don't just take anyone's word for it, they investigate, and they don't waste time doing so. I have just had my reason for living taken away from me and don't get any time to come to terms with that before being given an inquisition that has only the smallest level of empathy aligned with it. Obviously cops have some understanding of Sudden Infant Death Syndrome, and the fact that it is usually the cause in circumstances like this, but these two seem to consider it an opportunity to make names for themselves by creating a crime that never occurred.

For the first time ever, I was thankful for the arrival of Cleo's parents. I didn't notice Cleo contact them, but it was a good thing she had. As devastated as us, they still had that extra level of separation that allowed them enough composure to aid us at this time. I was close to losing it at the insensitivity of the police who barely allowed us those last moments before Olivia's lifeless body was taken away. We needed middle ground which thankfully Graham and Cheryl provided. In amongst the agony that Cleo and I were experiencing, it was also undoubtedly the most harrowing moments of their lives too, so I was grateful for their support and assistance with the police.

Olivia was nearly 12 months old, past the greatest stage of risk of SIDS. As a girl, she had a lower risk factor. She wasn't born premature, nor did she have any other infection that would have increased her risk. At this point, it was a one in a million possibility. Therein lies the suspicions that the police seem to have. What is sometimes seen as SIDS is later identified as another cause, such as suffocation, hypothermia or neglect. They will not find anything. I just need to grieve.

I don't recall when the police left us, but they were clear we'd have more dealings with them on the matter. Fortunately, the medical professionals on hand were more understanding. This wasn't a scene as unfamiliar to them as you'd like to believe. They understood nobody was more vulnerable than a parent who had just lost a child. Their expertise would confirm the cause of death and allow us to mourn as grieving parents should.

In those brief moments I had on my own, I realised why people might have felt a level of suspicion towards Cleo and me; we looked guilty because we felt guilty. Not guilty of any wrongdoing, but it's impossible not to feel guilty about every moment where we could have done something different. If only one of us had checked on her at the right moment this could have been avoided. Of course we couldn't know, but those realities disappear in this type of analysis. We both couldn't be more certain that we didn't warrant blame, but that didn't mean we couldn't bring ourselves to apportion blame to ourselves.

How could this happen? No warning. No indication of any possible problems. She was checked not long before she was found dead. At that point sleeping soundly and safely. We were so close the whole time.

The difference between Cleo and me was so more evident in the pain of this experience. I craved solitude for my grief while she needed physical proximity. I had to give her this despite the emotional expense on me. I couldn't pretend the loss was any less for her. She had carried Olivia for nine months;

how could I downplay that. A better couple would have loved and lost together, but in truth we had lost her individually. Any attempts to share the pain were effectively putting on a show. We were in truth both selfish with our pain. Both of us believed that nobody could grasp the level of our pain, not even each other.

She believes that I blame her. I believe that she blames me. I doubt either of us do this sincerely, but how does anyone best deal with tragedy? Grief is impossible to conquer, but blame has a natural combatant. Hate. Manufacturing that blame is ineffective. I know that her love was the same as mine. She did everything she could, as did I. There is no genuine blame either way, just overwhelming grief.

I don't know how long it will be before I can sleep again. I don't know when any of this will feel real. I don't see how I'll ever move beyond this. I've experienced things in life that have built a hard edge within me but that's been balanced by a softer side. Olivia encapsulated every element of that, and now she is gone. It's only the hardness that remains. A bitterness. An anger. I don't know where, when or how it will escape me, but the world as I saw it yesterday no longer exists.

CHAPTER 24

8.38am

Darkness didn't begin to explain what life had become. If all the struggles in my life had dug a hole for me, this had sunk me to a new depth. No tragedy can compare with losing your own child. Throughout life, I had looked at Matthew O'Connor as the epitome of tragedy. Suddenly I found myself walking in his shoes. Underground, dark, devastated, broken.

Every day we were exposed not just to the reminders of Olivia's life but the reminder of her death too. In the supposed safety of our home, and the sanctity of our bedroom, the place she drew breath for the last time was unavoidable. Each of us stayed in there for hours trying to contemplate how and why this could have occurred. That probably isn't quite what we did, for we were too numb to be processing any rational thoughts. One thing was certain, for all the hours we spent in that room over the ensuing few months, there were very few times either of us could sleep.

Cleo and I continued to cohabitate after Olivia's passing. We ate meals at the same table, lay in the same bed, yet we were strangers. I had been granted long term leave as there was no chance of me being able to function at work. For the ensuing period, my life was almost entirely spent at home, as was Cleo's. This proximity did little to aide our lack of closeness. Emotionally we were stuck on a path that never bended, and our descent fuelled further issues. The longer we spent in silence, the more we saw each other as opponents. It was as though we were in competition as to who was the most destroyed and that whoever reached out first would be admitting that they were the less broken. Neither of us was more or less broken than the other – how could such a measure ever be taken?

We had great assistance from our families and close friends. Naturally such a tragedy breaks a few people, but it shakes many more. Cleo had a lot more family and close friends than I did, so it happened that most of the assistance came from *her* people. When we were happily married and welcomed Olivia into the world, they were all *our* people. At the height of the turmoil we faced, there didn't seem to be any such thing as us. Everything was hers or mine. We were incapable of running errands, doing our shopping and normal day to day life so it was so often her family and friends stepping in to do this for us. All these people showed complete care and empathy to me. There was never any sense of me being excluded, but I already knew that Cleo and I wouldn't be able to overcome this. I knew that when the day came that we went our separate ways, these people would be at her doorstep helping to ensure that she recovered. Barely my name would be remembered.

As blurry as my memory of this period is, my recollection of timings is far from perfect. It was around April of the following year when the dynamics at home began to change.

Cleo was really beginning to show progress and change. She was a lot more animated with friends. Before long she began to communicate with me but not how I'd hoped. Whereas she had always been as non-confrontational as me, she was now speaking her mind. Usually this involved attacking me for not being at the same stage of recovery as she was. There was no consideration, just an attitude that reflected a view that *I'm this much better now so you need to be too.*

She went back to work in June, while I was still far from ready, despite a pending return date set for July. Being back at work seemed to invigorate her, and she started socialising more and finding more opportunities to enjoy life. I resented the advance she had made. How could she feel ok about anything so soon after losing Olivia? I know it wasn't soon and she hadn't forgotten but I remained in the same mode as months earlier where we virtually competed to be the most upset. I hadn't moved on at all. Seeing any sign of happiness from her upset me. I know that is wrong, but it is true.

Our arguments became more frequent though they always worked in the same way. She would attack me, and I would avoid the issue. I always refused to argue and retreated to another part of the house. Sometimes she would follow me and continue the attack while other times she would wait, knowing that I would be dwelling on what was coming to me later. Make no mistake, I am not suggesting that she was wrong to try and raise issues. Other than spend the next sixty years living in utter misery the only way forward was to start taking steps. She was ready and it was appropriate for her to do everything she could. I wasn't ready and couldn't accommodate her.

Throughout the problems that Cleo and I faced, I tried to reflect on what we were like before Olivia. We had always seemed happy, but possibly my memories were tainted by the realities that came later. I feel like we both settled in order to make it work. It's natural on a first date to hide your weaknesses and go out of your way to make a good impression. As relationships build, you let each other into more of the real picture. I'm not sure that Cleo and I really did this. No doubt there were negatives that couldn't stay hidden. I can dress to hide my oversized stomach, but eventually she had to see me with my shirt off. She was never going to look as good when she woke up as she did on our first date. These aren't the issues that compromise relationships, but they symbolise the deeper truths that we were even more intent to hide.

There are things that really challenge how you cope with others, be they lovers, family, friends or acquaintances. Where your interactions are minimal enough you learn to accept these things and move beyond them, but with a partner that isn't so easy. Cleo and I chose to try this rather than confront it in the early days. When things turned to shit, all these issues began to compound.

'I don't mind, you choose,' was a favourite phrase for both of us and applied to such a vast quantity of things. In our early days, even when we hated each other's choices, we were happy enough that our loved one had what they wanted. That tolerance, consideration, and willingness to put each other first had long disappeared. The *I don't mind, you choose* line still got used just as prolifically, but it was then always followed with a contemptuous response towards what that choice had been.

My father was hospitalised, and I flew to Adelaide for a few days. When I flew back Cleo seemed so unhappy to see me, that I wondered if there had been any point coming home. I put my suitcase in the boot, then jumped in the car. Before there was any form of greeting or a kiss on the cheek, I was subjected to her now familiar attitude and frustrations.

'You took your time,' she said in response to me being one of the last people from the flight to get out of the terminal. Normally absence should make the heart grow fonder, yet being apart hadn't even brought us a few minutes of respite from the tension. I felt things couldn't survive, I just couldn't foresee at that stage quite how they would end.

Throughout this period every issue that was raised was done so by Cleo. That, and my non-confrontational nature would form the reason that she was so shocked when I told her that I was leaving her. I told her, though not completely believing it, that I was proud of the way she was getting her life back on track. I focused on the fact that we were now in sufficiently separate places that we were both hindering each other more than we could possibly help. I suspect she was relieved. After all the trauma we had endured, and the pain that I was still not close to overcoming, she didn't want to be the villain to end the marriage. When I made the decision, she was saved from making it. She didn't make any attempts to stop me and I'm sure that she believed at that time, that my departure would be the best thing for her and an opportunity to build a new and better life.

It was three weeks from that night before I left. I had decided I would move back to Adelaide to be close to my father. I was sleeping in the spare room, and for the three weeks I was there Cleo and I had reached a new point of friendship. We were civil. Perhaps that even understates it. We went out of our way for each other for these three weeks knowing that there was nothing beyond that point of time we had to deal with for each other. Whenever there is a finish line in sight, anything seems more bearable. There was even a level of flirtation from her and an indication that she wanted me to rethink moving to Adelaide. She wouldn't commit to us, but she liked the idea of the convenience of me being just down the road. I knew that the only way each of us could ever move forward was to understand what was truly behind us. What we had endured had changed each of us, and the two new people who had taken the place of the old Anthony and Cleo, were not compatible.

Once I had settled in Adelaide, Cleo was in contact regularly, far more than anyone who was just a friend. She acknowledged she missed me and continually encouraged me to come back home so that we could try again. I knew that she missed the fantasy of our early days. I knew full well how far removed that fantasy was from reality. Bit by bit the contact dropped, and I heard that she had started dating someone. Once she knew I was aware she became less secretive in her social media, and I got to see just how quickly things were moving. I was happy for her, yet as someone who had been effectively alone since that fateful night, I did feel a hint of jealousy. I knew that my time of healing was continuing. Moving on with someone else would be a part of that, but it was not a part I was ready for.

Some wounds heal, but those that are severe enough can only heal so much. I think of Olivia as much as I did nine years ago when I had first moved back here. A major piece of my heart broke and can never be repaired.

The tragic ends of Antony and Cleopatra were meant to be their own, not that of their children. If we'd been cursed, why had the curse played out in such a way that the innocent party paid the price?

I dated a few times in the subsequent years but it was virtually impossible. With time and the experiences I'd lived through, I'd become even less able to function through social niceties. Where I had the greatest problem was with two women I genuinely did like. While that should have been exactly what I am looking for, it turned out more to be exactly what I fear. The sight of potential saw me project a future, and as soon as I did that I return overcome with grief to the memory of Olivia and the future as it should have been. I don't pretend it to be the right course of action, but like every other aspect of life I have given up on this as well.

Seven years on and Cleo is still with Darryl, the man she began dating soon after I returned to Adelaide. The time between each contact gets progressively greater, though as soon as we interact it is like when I first moved back here. That said, there is such a distinct lack of care and consideration that she shows for my wellbeing that I think she retains the contact for her own self-serving purposes. I wonder how she will react when she hears about today's events?

CHAPTER 25

8.40AM

In the 15 minutes since I left home, the skies have changed significantly. It still feels comfortable, but the dark clouds have rolled in. I'm hoping that I don't have delays between now and the sanctuary of the underground car park at work. My garden needs rain, and I enjoy it myself at suitable times, but not when I'm on my way to work. Provided it holds of for ten more minutes I am more than happy for a downpour.

Less than 200 metres from a major intersection, one of the lycra brigade flies past me. Seriously, why the fuck do people feel this need? The lights have just turned red, he is going to have to stop, why overtake people with the necessity of being the first to stop and the one to wait longest? Wherever my mind goes, I still monitor traffic enough to be conscious of what is around me. If speeding up will have me catching a set of lights, I do. If I am going to miss a set of lights, I decelerate from a reasonable distance. I don't understand the appeal of being stopped at the lights longer. In the case of the guys on road bikes in lycra, it is probably attention seeking more than anything. We have a small proportion of the number of bikes commuting that you'd see in Europe, yet the number of cyclists in lycra here is far higher. People driving to work don't wear motor racing overalls and helmets. I can't understand why cyclists here feel the need to be dressed like they're in a professional race. It's a goddamn commute.

I make comparisons with Europe quite frequently, as it has been my one point of solace. Since losing Olivia, I've barely a good memory outside of travelling. Not only Europe, but a couple of trips through the Middle East has seen me find value in life that has been impossible to find at home. Maybe it is the lack of travel since the global pandemic began that has seen me descend to my lowest point.

Before being on my own again I hadn't been overseas since the ill-fated trip to Fiji when I was an infant. Perhaps in part due to that trip, travel had never held any great appeal to me. Tom had convinced my mother to travel to the UK for a cousins wedding. I wasn't overly keen just a year on from Olivia's death, but I agreed to join her. She had done enough for me that it felt wrong to not step up and assist her, as she was at a stage where solo travel would be a challenge. While the wedding was something I could have done without, I enjoyed the rest of the trip. Seeing my brother for the first time since my wedding was better than I expected. We've never been close, but there wasn't the dominant older brother feel emanating from him anymore. Beyond him, experiencing the sights of London was amazing. I could easily have spent ten weeks without ever having a shortage of things to see and do. It was disappointing I didn't get to see more, but time was against me. From the moment I got back home, I was ready to start planning my next trip.

In the eight years since, I have managed one decent trip overseas each year, saving up every bit of available annual leave to use on travel. Each year when I tick a few more things off my bucket list, I replace them with a much larger set of additions. When I'm lost in the moment of thinking about these travels, I move away from the emotional trauma that defines most of my life. Sure enough, each time I return from a trip I have a couple of weeks of returning to normal before sinking to a deep depression. Post travel depression is real.

As I believe so strongly that we are the sum of all our experiences, I know that this sum really needs a few positives within the equation. Travel provides this for me in spades.

People would be stunned if they realised my financial position. How can I travel overseas so often if I have no money? The truth is that travel kept me alive. Without having the excitement of a trip to look forward to, I don't know how I would have retained any degree of sanity in the darkest days. So what if it has saddled me with debt, if it's been the only thing keeping me going, then that is a small price to pay. I doubt too many people would consider a suicidal outlook with money in the bank to be better. Not only has each trip uplifted me, but so much of the build-up has inspired positivity for an extended period. Whether it is the positivity of counting down the days to departure or the continual planning and studying of all my destinations, the actual trip is only part of the joy.

As a younger man I believed that I would be a husband and father while having a successful career in something with real meaning. My life would have worth, not just to me but to others. Reality has seen the direction change markedly.

Fatherhood was momentary. I was an ordinary husband. I am too old for a career to magically appear. I am stuck in a boring and meaningless public service job. Little amongst this generates significance, but travel provides it without obligation to commit to anything more than my desires.

If I was to be asked what I did six days ago, I would have enormous trouble telling you anything more than *I went to work*. Conversely if someone was to ask me what I did six years ago today, I could give them a much more thorough answer. *After waking early in my hotel room at La Defense, I made my way downstairs to the breakfast buffet and ate an obscene amount. I then ducked outside for a quick smoke before racing upstairs to get ready for my tour groups departure. Spending several hours on the bus including an hour on the side of the road due to mechanical issues, we eventually arrived in Lucerne. I wandered the downtown area for a while before hiring a pedal boat and going out onto Lake Lucerne and basking in the majesty of the surrounding mountains. After an unimpressive dinner at our hotel, I walked just under a kilometre to the Lucerne Casino where I spent 100 euro and lost the lot far quicker than I could believe. Unlike what I'd be inclined to do at home, I stopped at this point rather than reach a point I'd later regret. I stayed watching others gamble before settling in to watch some of the Champions League football semi-final. I engaged with people who didn't share a common language, yet we all still managed to communicate effectively. After this I made my way back to the hotel to sleep in a bed infinitely less comfortable than the one I'd had in Paris.* This was in no way a standout day on the road, but it symbolises the heightened experiences that occur through travel.

Years later I can remember every little piece of every day I have spent overseas. The experiences are so enriching that my senses take in the smallest details. I can feel myself completely back in the time and places whenever I reflect on them. People I have met once stay in my head. The smells and tastes of dishes I've eaten, including meals no better than ones I may have at home, are still so much more entrenched because the mind is so much more open to the experience.

I find myself constantly questioning whether life is all about the small set of magnificent experiences. The monotony of the everyday is something we endure while we prepare for the next great moment. Other times I consider the monotony is what life is about and the magic moments are just a distraction from real life. If the former is true, then surely the way to live is to maxmise the great moments. Stop trying to deal with the grind of life and start aiming for the pinnacle of life as frequently as possible. Each of us lives an average of 30,000 days in our life. Maybe we should stop focusing on extending our life span and reset our target to increase the number of days that matter. I doubt many people can look at more than 1% of their lives as having really mattered. 300 days for most people, though ask them to reflect on these and few could outline that many. Through travel, I'm way ahead of 300. I don't need to live long. I've lived hard. In many ways that's been bad, but on the road, I've tasted the other side.

Even though the days and weeks fly when travelling, trips can seem longer in the memory bank. I travelled through the Middle East for six weeks in 2017. The time flew like six days at the time, yet in my memory it feels like six months, as most of my 2017 memories are from that trip. Travelling in that region exposed me to a different life teaching me about humanity and what defines us. This is the perfect example of why travel adds so much to the equation of our lives. Travel teaches us without us trying to learn. We develop an understanding that there is a massive difference between 'life' and 'my life.' The life traumas that play their role in defining me aren't diminished, but seeing more of the world gives an additional level of understanding of where it fits in the scheme of life. Seeing people that have endured tragedies as soul destroying as I have, yet have picked up, moved on and grown from it is inspiring. Understanding difference between people and understanding the humanity that underpins opposite groups is the greatest education for life that I have ever been exposed to.

If the hole I live in has been dug through the course of my life, it seems that the only escape to the surface comes when I travel. I've tried to rekindle the feelings of the road at home but never successfully. Maybe I needed to live off the grid. Fake my death and runaway perhaps? I can't say I didn't consider it.

The sum of me includes the impact of every trauma I've lived through. It also includes the vast number of experiences and lessons that I have accumulated across the planet. Who cares if I can't pay my bills when I have seen the majesty of the Northern Lights dancing above me? Why worry about being alone when I have looked to the vastness of the skies from the Arabian Desert? All that I've seen has enriched me and inspired me to seek more. I can be at peace with the idea of my death, but far less at peace with an ongoing life that doesn't give me the growth, the joys and the experiences that travel has given me.

While I still feed off a myriad of recollections from travelling, the inability to do more in the past two years has stopped this catalogue of memories from growing. Travel is addictive and two years without a hit has had a massive impact on me.

When the pandemic hit it affected everybody. Working from home was a change, but insignificant in comparison with the travel restrictions. There was a noted mental health effect on people the world over. I found that having nothing to look forward to was crushing. It had taken a long time for me to find a form of salvation. Losing it impacted me severely.

Travel now comes with only the slightest of restrictions, yet I haven't been able to seriously contemplate it. The last two years have thrown up situations where just as it seems like normality was ready to return, it was taken away again. Planning has led to plans being broken and the time spent looking forward to something special, being destroyed.

When the present distresses us too much, there is only the reminiscing of the past or the hope in the future that keeps us going. Throughout life, the past has never been my friend, so I've clung tightly to hope. As that has faded from its previous place of safety for me, I have little left.

I think ahead to what awaits me sooner. Work. A place where hope has not existed for a long time. I really should have found a way of doing something about that, but it takes action, one of my many great weaknesses. As I slow down for the red light, I wait behind the lycra hero for the lights to change. How pointless his desperate rush was.

CHAPTER 26

TUESDAY APRIL 5, 2016

Punctuality has never been a strength of mine. Five minutes late here. Ten minutes late there. Today I have realised that I am twenty years late on this particular expedition.

Travel seems to be the domain of two groups; those in their early twenties having a gap year, and those in their early sixties who have just retired, got rid of their children and are making the most of life while still fit enough. Here I am, half-way between the two. I regret not having travelled when I was younger. So many amazing experiences. So much to learn that enriches life back home. So much more life I could have lived, but wasted. Regrets are futile. There is so much to gain each day now, so it is wasteful reflecting on opportunities not taken in the past. Learn the lesson from it, then move on. My lesson is not what I should have done in the past. The lesson is what I should do in the future.

My aunt Sarah travelled extensively with her husband Leon. He didn't seem to have a redeeming quality, at least that I ever saw. In hindsight, paying for the trips may have been one good thing he did, but I'm sure there was little else.

Sarah wrote extensively detailed letters whenever they were away and made the places and the experiences sound idyllic. It made me yearn to explore these places the way she had. These yearnings didn't last though. By the time they arrived home, the stories that didn't make the letters began to come out. None of these involved anything bad about the places or the people they interacted with. It was all Leon.

He complained about every experience he had, diminishing every positive experience Sarah had. None of this stopped him, as he was constantly working on plans for the next trip. Travel complaints clearly got him more attention than regular complaints, and that seemed to be at the forefront of his wish list. He would spend tens of thousands of dollars on a trip yet would create additional hassles over a few dollars in parts of it. Departure day always meant Leon drove Sarah to the train station leaving her with all their baggage on the platform. He then returned the car home and walked back to the station. They caught the train halfway to the airport where they transferred to a crowded cross-town bus, carting multiple suitcases up and down steps and across the road. This came with a cost of one dollar each as opposed to forty dollars in a taxi. It cost them an additional two hours and a stack of wellbeing, but that didn't matter. No, a taxi would have been a waste of money in his eyes, despite them both being written off for the first day, thanks to this ridiculous saga.

Once getting to the airport, Leon remained a pain in the arse. In fairness, he would have been the same at home. At least for Sarah, the time abroad meant everything else was good.

Whenever I thought back on these trips, it was Leon's bullshit that stood in my mind. When the opportunities to travel came up, I associated it with the experiences Sarah had; amazing, but with a huge chunk of aggravation. Being far less patient than her, I wasn't satisfied that this combination was for me. The obvious solution was travelling on my own, but I'd been so turned off the idea of travel thanks to Leon that I lost sight of the other side of the equation.

Two years ago I went to London for just over a week. I travelled with my Mum and met up with my brother Tom. We attended our cousins wedding, but most of the time I was just an ordinary tourist. Mum was born and raised in London and knows the city well enough to not feel bound by a need to see everything. I've therefore spent a lot of my time exploring on my own. It was amazing, but more than the experiences I had in the week, I felt an overwhelming change in my view of travel. I realised how narrow my world had been. I needed to go further, go deeper and really start discovering the world and my place in it. I went back to the UK and Ireland last year and the hook was deeper in me.

Last time I was part of a group, but this time I'm all alone. Testing my boundaries even further, I'm now across the channel in Paris. This is my first time outside of the English-speaking world and for it to be in a city as complete as this is a dream come true. I'm continually losing myself but that isn't a bad thing; it ensures finding so much more. There is a happiness within that I don't recall feeling since Olivia left us. It may be fleeting, but with every new revelation the city offers me, I feel something new stir within my soul. Discovery inspires me. Travel may well be the missing ingredient in my life, or at least one that I can do something about.

I have been here for a week, and it is without doubt the best week I have had since her loss. The past seven days seem to have blended into one perfect experience. I say that, though of course it hasn't been always perfect. That is part of the appeal. Life, as nobody knows better than me, is never all good. When it appears too good to be true, it is generally a sign that it isn't true. Some people may enjoy basking in the joy of an allusion. I like to know that I am not about to wake up from a dream and into a darker reality.

Tomorrow I get the train from Gare de L'est to Strasbourg where I'll spend a couple of days before moving on to a couple of weeks around Germany and the same again in the Netherlands and Belgium. I then join a tour group back in London that will take me through Switzerland and Italy before I go home.

I am journaling my experiences every day. Perhaps inspired by the letters my aunt wrote which first brought an understanding of how great the experience of travel can be, I am ensuring that I have something more than just a memory of the moments. Within each day there are moments that blow me away, and while I know I will remember the gist of what I saw and did on my travels, will the details slowly disappear from my memory? Perhaps. By having detailed descriptions of all that I do, I will be able to look back on today in half a century and see why I ended the day a better person than I started it.

In the morning I had gone walking, and without knowing quite how I got there, found myself at Gare Saint-Lazare, one of the city's major train stations. A woman was lost, and desperately seeking assistance. She was speaking English, though with a thick Eastern European accent. Although most Parisians can speak a little English, they tend to save this for when it is in their advantage to use it. Although I was only able to give her basic directions to her hotel in Les Halles, she had a starting point. In a city where I was losing myself, I was able to assist someone worse off than me. It felt good to do something with no personal gain.

As it turned out, there was a gain. Walking out of the station, I passed a woman sitting out the front of a café. She called me over, saying it was refreshing to see someone help when everyone else just passed the person by, and offered to buy me a coffee. We talked. She told me plenty about Parisian life and I talked about life in Australia. For all the understanding that one can get walking the streets as a tourist, there is far more to learn about a city when you live like a local. When she invited me home with her, I was given the most enjoyable lesson of my life.

Jene-Marie was quite the host, though I was genuinely as interested in the insight she gave me to local life as anything else. She lived in a tiny apartment on the Rue de Vienne that consisted of a bed, a bathroom and a tiny kitchen and living area.

'This is why we spend our life in the community not in our apartments. Many of us eat most of our meals out. There is no space to buy anything that needs to be stored. What we consume at home is brought fresh from our local grocer or boulangerie. You see them on every block as most of us don't have cars, for there is nowhere to park them.'

She said we must go out to lunch. Whether she was trying to get rid of me or not, she took me back closer to my hotel.

We ate at Les Volcans on the Rue de Faubourg. She taught me another piece of French life, the long lunch. Businesspeople sat at tables near us, and everyone took their time over three courses and wine.

'Lunch is not a break in the workday, it is a priority of the day which work has to fit around.'

We went our separate ways after lunch. For a tourist with no set plans, this was a memorable and unexpected experience. For a local woman who'd slipped out for a mid-morning coffee, I wondered how abnormal the day turned out. Perhaps this too was a feature of Parisian life.

Mid-afternoon I walked down the Boulevard de Magenta. There were groups congregating on the sidewalk that didn't look overly friendly, and I made it my mission to walk quickly on to better surrounds. Just after this I saw an incredibly attractive young woman. She smiled at me and said a strongly accented 'Hello.' I was about to stop and say 'Bonjour,' feeling charmed that such a pretty young lady would initiate contact so directly in the street. I remembered my fundamental rule; if it seems too good to be true, it is too good to be true. This girl was bait, and the groups congregating near her were ready to pounce when she drew me to her. I put my head down and moved fast. I always carried a fake wallet when travelling, to hand over in case I run into trouble. Most likely this is what would have happened, but you can never be sure how such things will play out. Maybe without the pleasure of the morning, I may have been more susceptible to the trap that was set in the afternoon.

In the evening I found a brasserie on the Rue La Fayette, and after starting with a drink, got the attention of others by the bar courtesy of my accent. A group of locals were drinking there, but it included a couple of expat-Australians. What I had intended to be a quiet evening, with just a meal then a return to my hotel, ended up as a long and wonderfully entertaining night.

I could live another fifty years and I will remember the pieces of today. Tomorrow may have far less memorable elements, but I will remember it too as the one day I ever see Strasbourg for the first time. That is travel. There is always something new.

For all I have lost in life, so long as I am just a flight from new horizons, there will always be something to find.

CHAPTER 27

8.42AM

It is hard to snap out of fantasies about Europe. It is hard to snap out of the reality of Europe each time I return home. As much as I love it there, it is not so much the place or the lifestyle but the feeling I have when I am there. The experiences I get when I travel wouldn't give me the same feeling if they were everyday ones. The power of the moment lies in its scarcity. It is precious when it is rare. When travelling, every moment feels that way.

Life needs balance. You can't fully appreciate the good without the bad. In principle, the love I have for travelling would infer that I'd be happiest spending all of my time travelling. In practice nothing could be further from the truth. The thrill I get from the adventures on the road are the counterbalance to the mundane nature of life as a low-level public servant. The culture that inspires me offsets the wasteland that is not necessarily synonymous with this city, but with my place in it. It isn't Adelaide that is the problem. Base myself in Paris, and it will become the familiar scourge of monotony while Adelaide would provide the promising flicker of something different.

My stop at the lights has been extended. The lights have remained red, as fire brigades have come through the intersection. I haven't seen or smelt smoke anywhere, so I don't know what's going on, but traffic has been stopped for them. As always, the sight of them makes me feel uncomfortable. I was too young at the time to have clear memories of that fateful Ash Wednesday, but I have something potentially more dangerous. I remember remembering. As children, we have a natural propensity to exaggerate situations in our mind. Our memories, however they seem, actually reflect how we captured the moment in our heads, not how it happened. These images are then smeared further by the impact of time. However clearly I look back on moments like those days, the reality would have looked far different.

When the second Ash Wednesday fires tore through the Adelaide Hills in 1983, we were well and truly settled into our new home. At that stage, there was still a freshness to all we'd experienced. Coming on that of all days, the 1983 fires were more severe. The memories flooded back naturally, but even without what we knew, the media coverage was initially based heavily on the coincidence of the day.

I don't know what I experienced in 1980. I have a clear memory of 1983 which was dominated by the thought back to 1980 and the fear that had been born at that time. I know that ever since, I feel a shudder go through me at the thought or the sight of the same type of disaster. I'm not hamstrung for an ongoing period, but it was like a chill go through me as the fire brigades past through the intersection.

While I'd waited at the lights thinking of my earliest childhood memory, Lycra man didn't wait. He went through the red light when he could see it was safe. Should cars do that? Should lycra man break any other laws that suit him, if he happens to judge that it is safe for him to do so? Riding a bike is not just good for yourself, it is better for everyone. Society would benefit enormously if half of the cars on the road were replaced with bikes. Unfortunately, the reputation we all get is ruined by the considerable proportion of cyclists who act like dicks on the roads.

I'm forced to begin the Aussie salute as it is colloquially known. Flies are an incredibly common part of Australian life and although they tend to be far less prevalent on cool mornings like this, once you have one around your face there is a lot of swatting to be done.

This intersection is the half-way point of my ride. I'm not sure how accurate that is distance wise but more relevant is the change of scene that is apparent once this road is crossed. Prior to this point, it is typical Adelaidean suburbia, but once getting across this intersection, I will be riding through the parklands, the green dividing line between city and suburbs.

With the light now green, I make my way through the intersection. While initially I am still on a busy road, the surrounds are sufficiently different that my mind often transitions at this point. The tranquillity of the green space doesn't necessarily translate to greater peace of mind. More frequently it is at this point that my mind starts to tick over to work mode.

I've worked for the same government department for

seven years and I don't know how that has happened. Initially I had a contract for three months which seemed quite ideal, as the role didn't seem inspiring enough to justify a longer stay. Before too long, I won permanency. Without the need to find greener pastures, I fell into the trap of staying longer than served my best interests. My branch isn't the worst place to work, but stay long enough and you become jaded. Once you reach that point you feel yourself continually on a slide. I've changed roles a couple of times, but it has only ever been moving from one chair to another. It provides the feeling that you have swapped spokes but remain on the same wheel. The view remains identical.

Morale in our workplace is horrendous. It's never been good, but it is becoming progressively worse. It shouldn't be that way, but the little failings of each individual seem to combine into an aggregated failing that is large. Everyone considers the blame lies with someone else, but that's the one bit of common ground. I suppose that is the story of life; nobody considers themselves to be the bad guy. Management thinks staff are to blame for the lack of morale. Staff consider management to be out of touch and responsible for everything that is wrong. I've acted in a management position but have generally been a step below. I've had a foot in both camps. Like most things in life, placing the blame on the other side of the fence is easier than accepting any responsibility. It also stands in the way of ever resolving the issues.

Why is conflict so common? Every conflict has a hero and a villain, but which character is which depends on the angle you're watching from. We all like to think it's because the person who disagrees with us is the problem, but they're sitting back thinking the same about us. People are so reluctant to look at scenarios from another's perspective. By looking from the other persons view, and through communicating clearly, life can become so much easier. Certainly in our workplace this would eliminate the problems that plague us, yet nobody seems to rectify it. Who am I to talk when it comes to communication? Who would have the slightest insight into what goes on between my ears?

What do we do? It doesn't matter, as management only looks within an overly narrow focus. Follow standard operating procedures. Exceed individual key performance indicators. Obey governmental process guides. More of our salary budget is spent paying people to monitor performance than paying people for the actual performance. We seem to be at the forefront of 1990's management techniques, albeit a quarter of a century late to the party. Progressive economies have advanced, but we have failed to learn their lessons. While public service departments should become more efficient, we have become fatter. Management focus on restructures that deliver pay rises to themselves, while culling people at the bottom. They produce a net saving which earns the tick of approval at higher levels, but the greater costs are ignored. Staff are put under more pressure to perform individually, but the branch seems to face no evaluation of its overall performance. As a branch, we do less each year, and spend more to do it.

My role is bureaucratic. I produce very little. I filter work from management to the floor, then back, all while monitoring and measuring everyone below me. I'm frequently berated for the methods I use to get things done. My focus has always been on the big picture rather than the inefficient steps in a process. I don't care if you fail to meet a benchmark, if your work saves extra wasted hours fixing mistakes. Sam will then usually follow with a complaint that I haven't punished the good worker. We then have the same debate again.

The work we do is uninspiring. Feeling positive about the workplace is heavily dependent on the working relationships you have. We have a large enough workforce that it is almost guaranteed that you will have people you do and don't get along well with. How significant it is when you don't get along with people tends to define your view of the place. For most of my time here, the people I tended to find difficult were not significant enough to have a major impact on me. Over the past year, Terry and Sam have ensured that this has changed.

Most people have little idea how other perceive them. We often believe we know what people think, but how accurate we are varies. I think I have an idea, but I mock others who say that, so I shouldn't get too carried away about my view. I suspect that the opinions most people at work have of me are based around the lie of who I am. They piece together what they see and think it is a confident, intelligent, funny and positive man they work with, whether that is someone they like or not. The reality is I'm none of those things. There are so many other things that truly define me. Nobody I work with has any idea person is sitting amongst them.

'Who do you think is the staff member most likely to go postal here?' Patrick asked in a management meeting a couple of years back when we were both acting section managers.

'Other than me?' I asked maintaining a serious look which drew a laugh from everyone. I took that as a reasonable indication that nobody thought too much about my mental health issues. I knew that the correct answer was me. I remembered Renee and the knife. Yes, that didn't involve any harm being done, but I was a teen. I've had a lot more happen to drive the bitterness, anger and cynicism since then. While they argued between Chester, Sonia, Dmitri, and Brad, I knew none of them would doubt me if they happened to know more of my story. I've appeared an open book in my time here, but I've never discussed any of the big issues in my life. I wondered how much of my story I could share before they really started to worry about what laid beneath.

I have never committed the slightest act of violence in my life. I've never hit anyone, not even in the relative freedom of the sporting field where such things can be done discreetly. The frustrations at work over the years have certainly made me wish I could. The thought of walking into the office and causing carnage makes me smile, but then I think of each individual and really hate the thought of anything bad happening to them. Even Terry. There is a side to him that angers me beyond belief, but I feel like he's buried in a hole that's not too dissimilar to mine. In the same way that a paedophile warrants no sympathy if they had been victims themselves, I don't feel like Terry can be given a free pass because of his issues. I don't get a free pass for mine. I cop whatever is thrown at me, with no consideration for all I've endured. I don't wish him ill, I just wished he was gone.

I always clung to hope Sam would disappear from our workplace. She is all the subtlety that Terry lacks. That may sound like a compliment, but it is more a recognition of her calculating ways. If only she used her powers for good.

I suspect she thinks she does. There is so much more to her story that I will never know, but she has a hold over some powerful people that allows her to act with contempt for rules, regulations and good sense. I wouldn't want her blood spilt, but having blood on her hands seems reasonable. I wonder how she will deal with what is coming. Probably the same sort of fake niceties as always.

A few weeks back we had our annual building evacuation. Shortly afterwards I had a dream where all the staff were evacuated due to a bomb scare, only for a bomb to explode at our evacuation point, killing most of the people who work in our building. I was the primary suspect, as I was the only person who'd been in the building but failed to go to the evacuation point. I maintained my innocence. My cynicism had indicated that the only reason someone would ring up with a bomb threat against the building would be to round up everyone into one small area. From there, it would be a much easier and more accessible target for their vengeance. Naturally, I steered clear of that place, not because I was responsible, but because I had the foresight to act on reason. Explaining it to the police became a problem, as there was nobody who could understand the meaning of the word, reason.

My plans for today were nothing like the dream. They would ensure that Sam, Terry, and all those who played their games would be safe. They would however be left in no doubt of just how dark it was in the hole they'd helped bury me in.

CHAPTER 28

8.43AM

Riding this same route every day has meant that I have become so aware of the cycles of traffic lights that I barely need to look at them. Having stopped at the last intersection, it wouldn't matter how fast I rode, the next set of lights would turn green before I got there. They will stay green sufficiently long that I can ride my slowest and still catch the lights. I deliberately go slow. Further down the road I have to get across traffic to cut through the parklands. While the flow of traffic is so strong it means stopping and waiting, but if these lights change just after I pass, I can retain momentum and cross quickly and easily. Sometimes a cyclist gets stuck behind me at this point, frustrated by how slow I am. Two hundred metres down the road, they wait at the curb to get across the road and see me already on the other side. The tortoise again beats the hare.

My patience with people has deteriorated markedly over time. It is these little moments on my ride to work that aggravate me far more than they should. Why do I care if someone else doesn't read the traffic flow? It has no impact on me. I think that it is about something else altogether. Failure to look ahead and plan the most efficient options is of great significance in many areas of life. I spend so much time witnessing decision making that is reactive rather than proactive, that witnessing it on the commute has become an aggravation.

Every person offers us something new and something that can add value to our lives. Detecting what this is and avoiding the crappy side of a person isn't always so easy.

Meeting people is a wonderful thing. Interacting with people we don't know educates us and helps us grow. It exposes us to different aspects of life and we are richer for it. Building these interactions into ongoing relationships is a whole other step and one that I lack the inclination to participate in. Perhaps that is where my love of travel stems from. Meeting new people who you're unlikely to see again ticks all my boxes.

Every year human civilisation becomes more urbanised. Our cities become more densely populated each year to further push us all together. Greater exposure to others doesn't seem to provide greater understanding of others. Disunity is more common than ever. The closer together we are forced, the further apart we drift. More conflict. More intolerance.

I nearly choke at the principle of national pride. There are so many divisive issues in our society. Our national day, our national anthem and our national flag are all caught up amongst these. I'm not too concerned one way or the other on any of these issues, but I cannot for the life of me see how those reluctant to change cannot see why the causes for division exist. We cannot truly unite underneath principles that we don't share. I doubt we will ever share a real national identity, but I think few countries in the 21st century do. National identity is a convenient folktale for politicians to sell to their people, but how real is it? When did you last see the people of this country really come together? The closest you see is through sport. We may all claim to have felt pride through Cathy Freeman, the Socceroos or the Paralympic team, but walk down the street the day after their triumphs and the same people who wouldn't previously make eye contact with you, still didn't. If these sporting triumphs had genuinely united us, we would share that feeling. We never shared it. We each took our quota of joy and experienced it individually and separately.

I remember in 2020, the echoes around the nation that said we were all in the pandemic together. *Help each other. Work together.* What crap. Walking into supermarkets where the shelves had been stripped, as people panic bought and acted on selfishness left a hollow ring to our shared experience. To most people, any fellow Australian you didn't know, didn't matter. There is some level of community evident at a more micro level, but then the same can be seen anywhere. It isn't something where our whole nation unites, but small linked components within it. Nationhood itself is the sale of a myth.

We have an election at the end of this week. Each party highlighting the flag or other national symbols to make us feel patriotic and remind us why *they* are the ones fighting for what our nation really is and needs. Posters and signs are everywhere. I'm sure by the end of this ride I will passed more than a thousand. If only as much work was put into policy as they put into promotion, maybe we'd see progress.

It hardly matters, most Australians will continue to support their own longstanding view. We divide again into all our parts before the winner stands up and says that they are there for everyone.

We show compassion in times of crisis. Through fire and flood, most Australians have shared a desire to help each other. But that same attitude is common amongst us when we see global tragedies unfold as well. The empathy for Ukraine is as common here as it would be for Australian victims of tragedy. The same shared view is felt with each mass-shooting in American schools. A world away, yet humanity unites us, not nationality.

I'm a middle-aged single male public servant living in a mid-sized city. I have more in common with a middle-aged single public servant in Birmingham, Berlin, Beirut, or Bloemfontein than I have in common with a farmer in Longreach, a millennial in inner-Sydney or a corporate chief in Perth. Nationality doesn't unite us, commonality does. People rarely choose to look for commonality, they just thrive on it when it finds them.

How much I can relate to different people seems to be diminishing. After Olivia's death I began drinking as a coping mechanism. Who could blame me? Of course, what sometimes starts as a justifiable source of assistance can end up as a highly dangerous addiction. I don't know how long it took before it became a problem and how much longer before I accepted it as such. With time it progressed from occasional excess when I felt low, to drinking excessively every day.

My descent to alcoholism took years. At my lowest point the ride to work was even more important as it was the one point of the day that my mind and body were receiving relief from the punishment I was putting them through. I still had to stop on the way in for a smoke, but it was as healthy as my day would be. A few bad days at work had seen me have a drink or two at lunch after which I coped with the afternoon better. This led to drinking more frequently at lunch until too many of the problems at work were ruining my mornings. I then began slipping spirits into my coffee cup and getting a reasonable amount of juice into my system early in the day.

My descent was slow enough that it was never obvious to other staff. People saw me under the influence, but inebriated Anthony was normal Anthony in the eyes of my colleagues. There were times when suspicions were aroused, but generally people just put my behaviour down to it being me. *That's just Anthony.* I was always capable of riding home at the end of each day, so I wasn't ever too drunk. In all fairness I would have failed a breathalyser test most days, but those tests are designed for people driving killing machines, not people on the relative safety of a bike. My chances of killing someone were high, but it was only myself placed under threat.

Often enough I'd stop to drink on the way home and would be a real mess by the time I got home. There were many occasions when I woke up wondering how I would get to work that morning, not realising that my bike was in the backyard. I'd have ridden home when far too wasted to have any recollection of those rides. I have no idea how I kept making it home, but time after time I'd be there, often sleeping in the backyard, too uncoordinated to get my key in the door.

Drinking never brought many real positives. I wasn't commonly socialising while drinking, I was just really using alcohol as a silencer of my mind. It worked to some extent, as I found that I was less caught in depressing thought after a few drinks. Once I continued a step too far, I'd become more entrenched than ever in the debilitating memories of the past. From that point, only annihilation of my mind through drinking beyond consciousness helped. In the late 2010s this was how most nights ended.

Eventually, early in 2019 when I was at my previous lowest, I reached a point where I felt so sick, so consistently, that I gave up almost without trying. I was taking more days off work and often didn't drag myself out of bed all day. The effort of getting more to drink was too much. I almost took comfort from the misery I felt when sobering up. My self-hatred had reached a point where I was less interested in easing my pain and had an appreciation for how much I deserved to suffer. I still drank to excess on the occasions I started, but I felt less compelled to start. Without a conscious plan, I realised at one point that I had gone a week without a drink. It was only at that point that I set a determined goal to keep that going. Although I was dealing with a burgeoning level of depression, I felt a sense of satisfaction when I reached three months sober. Life felt no better, yet somehow I seemed to have gained enough self-respect to continue.

Being mentally coherent day and night was destined to have impacts both positive and negative on me. I no longer had the ability to escape the tragedies of the past when they dominated my mind, but at the same time they seemed to take residence there much less frequently. The pit remained as dark as it had ever been, but each cause of the darkness seemed to take its place in less confronting ways. Media stories of paedophilia had me recounting my experiences with Mr. Harris just as before, but at least it now required that sort of trigger. When I was drinking, he would appear in my mind from nowhere. Olivia took place there more frequently, both before and after my sobriety, but my ability to deal with the pain had improved.

As an alcoholic I frequently wished I was dead. As a sober man I rarely felt glad to be alive. The difference was subtle, but life at least now seemed like the default position. Unfortunately, as the problem of alcoholism disappeared it merely saw other addictions become more overpowering. The happiest people are those who learn best from their mistakes. I was a dismal failure at this, as I never conquered a problem without inviting a similar one to take its place.

CHAPTER 29

WEDNESDAY MARCH 20, 2019

Arseholes. They throw me out of here so often, but they always let me back in the next day. When it suits them, they're happy to take my money, but once they think they're getting no more out of me, they couldn't give a shit. Responsible service of alcohol, my arse. Money talks, and bullshit walks. If I got run over out the front of this place, the staff would run out, fossick through my pockets and grab my wallet long before even considering calling an ambulance.

I planned to stay for just a quick drink. It's been a bad day and because I was able to remember too much of it, I stayed, continuing to drink until I forgot. It wouldn't have been an issue if it wasn't for Jerry, this old bastard who hangs around here like a bad smell. He's the one who provokes me with the rubbish he talks about. We get animated and eventually it goes too far. Same thing happens every time we're both in here. I guess it's my fault for not finding another place to drink, but it's just too convenient between work and home.

Tonight, Jerry started going on about the shootings in the mosque in Christchurch last week.

'It was all part of a conspiracy. A false flag. Supposedly a right-wing extremist kills a bunch of Muslims because that's what he believes in, but who gains? The opposite side. They act like that Jacinda is a saint, the Muslims get a whole lot of sympathy and the right wing look insane. Their government were behind the whole thing.'

'That's fucking insane,' I said. I'd been drinking for several hours and although very drunk, there was no impairment on my ability to decipher the level of crap he was sprouting.

'You just believe everything the government and the main-stream media tell you Anthony, right.'

'I believe the fucking evidence,' I said. 'Sometimes governments hide things. Sometimes the media gets things wrong. Usually, the official story is right. Every bit of evidence in this case suggests it is.'

'Of course. They're not amateurs. When they conspire, they make it look convincing otherwise it would defeat the purpose.'

He went on to talk about Sandy Hook and Port Arthur, suggesting they too were conspiracies designed by the anti-gun lobbies in their respective countries. I've always believed that you only needed to get upset with intelligent arguments, for it was these that could influence others to follow. Jerry offered nothing remotely intelligent in anything he said, yet I found myself unable to keep my composure with his crap.

'Just fuck off,' I said, finally losing my patience with him. Unfortunately, by this time I'd been drinking long enough that I was very loud in expressing my contempt towards the old fool. As I saw Mick, the publican walking towards me I knew what was coming. I never fought it. Mick was massive.

With a hand tied behind his back, he could pick me up and throw me across the road.

'When you gonna learn Anthony,' Mick said. 'A shit like Jerry ain't got any other options in life. You do. You might be good for business, but I'd rather see you be good for yourself.'

Riding home was the next issue. It took nearly five minutes to get the lock off my bike. I know the combination well enough but coordinating all the spots is bloody difficult. Still, getting on and staying on will be harder. I should've left it locked here, then come and got it after work tomorrow. Maybe not. If I had to come back here, the night would end up going the same way.

Shit. I didn't even make it to the corner. Moving slow is the hardest bit. I was going to have a chronic headache in the morning, now you can add bruising too. I didn't even feel myself falling until I hit the ground. I felt it then. Tomorrow I will feel it far worse.

What do I say if I ring up sick? I'm battered and bruised, and I don't know how? They'll know how, and they're not going to think too good of self-inflicted sick leave without pay. I don't have any other leave allocations left. I'll have to go to work.

I walk with my bike across the road and into the start of the parklands. The timing is good as I need to throw up. I chuck my bike down and heave. Then again. And again. I am so damned sick of doing this to myself, but the alternative of sobriety isn't any better. Usually I feel better once I've vomited, but it's taking its time to have that impact. I'm going to lay here just for a moment until I feel able to stand up again and get back on my bike.

As sure as my quick drink turned into something more, so too did my quick lay down. I don't know how long I was out for, but I know I'd slept for a little while. My bike was still beside me, and as I felt around so too was my wallet and my phone. Checking the time, it was 3.14am, so I must have slept for several hours. Although there's not too many people wandering the parklands at night, I'm surprised nobody disturbed me or stole from me in that time. They probably saw the drying pool of vomit around me and thought whatever they'd get away with wasn't worth it.

I must leave home in five hours and do it all again. I need to get home first. I can't keep doing this, but I can't work out how to stop.

CHAPTER 30

8.44AM

There is a little section in the parklands where there is some seating under a gazebo that gives minor protection from the elements. Every morning I see a subset of the same group of homeless people sitting in there, waiting until it is break-fast time at the nearby charity shelter. I used to look at them and contemplate how long it would be before I joined them. Although it's not so relevant now, there was a stage where financial disintegration appeared inevitable. Yeah, I owned my home, or at least I co-owned it with the bank that held my mortgage, but that fact belied a bigger picture that made the long term look shaky.

Five years ago I was quite secure. I had money in the bank, manageable debt and while hating my job, I was looking at the prospect of building wealth as quickly as possible. I was hoping to facilitate retirement as soon as possible, ideally by now. This meant taking risks and every risk I took was the wrong one. For two years I lost a lot of money in shares, commodities and derivatives and cut heavily into my savings. My almost permanent state of drunkenness didn't help my decision making, but it was only after I stopped drinking that a bigger problem arose.

As things got worse, I took bigger risks and eventually moved away from investment markets and started gambling heavily. I have always been a bit of a gambler, so there was no big step to raise the stakes a little further. The problem was that something had changed in me. I wasn't gambling as a bit of a fun activity as I'd done in years gone by, but as a desperate move to improve my financial position. Years earlier I had developed a disciplined betting platform that returned consistent profits. Although the percentage of profit I made on turnover was small, the ability to maintain this offered an opportunity of escape from the working life which felt like it was killing me.

I did the sums. With a 3% profit on turnover, I could make the half a million dollars I needed by turning over $17million. Of course, with limited funds available, that meant about 170,000 bets of $100 each. To do this in 3 years, which already seemed way too slow, I needed to make eleven hundred bets a week. I had to go beyond the obvious. I needed to bet all through the night on events from around the world. I couldn't afford to keep missing opportunities. I wouldn't have time to socialise, nor would I have time to sleep properly. I was on a mission.

I kept this behaviour up for more than a year despite achieving nothing but losses. I had done the sums, I knew my theories would work, except once they are extrapolated to different events, the results didn't hold the same way. Betting on a horse race when I knew each horse inside out was one thing. Betting on horses on the other side of the world that I had never heard of would never provide the same consistently accurate results. I used mathematics to forecast sport, but when I didn't understand sports like football and tennis, my maths alone didn't give me the results I needed to turn profits. I had too much faith in my methods and kept betting bigger to recoup losses. All I achieved were bigger losses.

I was an addict.

I was pulling over three times on the ride to work to put another bet on. I would spend much of my day at work in the bathrooms putting more bets on or checking results and scores. I was waking up at 3am and betting on American racing until I couldn't keep my eyes open any more. Every now and then a betting company would tell me that they'd noticed a change in my betting and that I should assess if I had any sort of gambling concern. Five minutes later they would send me an email with another promotion designed to encourage me to bet more. The amounts I was pouring into accounts meant that there could be no question about whether betting was mere recreation. Recreational gamblers do not put bets on in each of 24 consecutive hours. They don't repeat this behaviour day after day.

I didn't stop. Once I had blown everything I had, I started betting with debt and maxed out both of my credit cards. I got another loan and more cards until they were maxed out too. By this stage it was no longer about money. I didn't have enough to be able to win any decent sums anyway. But I craved and needed that adrenaline that came with a winner. Losing $5000 in a session hurt, but even the feeling of a $10 win would be the first little fix to making me feel alright. Naturally that fix didn't hold me and I would need to reinvest that $10 in search of something stronger. Almost every time this continued until I was cleaned out again.

There were hundreds of times when I would remind myself that there was only two ways the story could end; complete self-destruction or quitting. I knew this as fact, yet every time I had that conversation in the desperate lows that followed a binge, the light of a new day saw the same old impulses feeding my brain.

Just a $20 profit, twenty sessions per week will get you back twenty thousand in a year. You know how easy this is, you merely have to avoid the ill-disciplined approach that has hurt you previously. Even though I'd faced this situation so many times before, I still found myself having the same internal debate. Merely avoiding ill-discipline was like suggesting living without oxygen. I couldn't be in that environment without ill-discipline controlling me, however much I wanted to believe it. Repeatedly when the inner voice spoke loud enough, I would deposit more funds. From there, I would get a winner or two to boost my balance and then proceed on a losing run until every cent was gone. Often out of outrage I would then deposit more to get back what I had lost. The fact that I had been winning at first was the lesson I'd take from the experience, telling me that I can do the same thing tomorrow but just be smarter by stopping when in front. That was something I physically couldn't do, yet also hadn't found a way of understanding why.

Everybody has read stories about compulsive gamblers who have stolen or embezzled to feed their habits. People get outraged by these stories and I'm not going to suggest they shouldn't, but it is so badly misunderstood. I've been addicted to a few substances but none of them come close to the power that a gambling addiction carries. I swear that an addict mid-gambling session has far less control than a person driving a car at ten times the legal blood alcohol reading. As a society we understand drug addiction and we understand the impact of alcohol and drugs on our capacity, yet we look at gambling as a question of willpower. We force companies to say 'Gamble responsibly' when such a thing is completely beyond the control of the very people who need to do so.

The gambling world has transformed so much in a generation. I grew up with racing in my blood, and as a young man I would go to the races or a betting shop and take a disciplined approach to trying to find winners. The opportunities were limited, and once the last race was run it was time to go home and plan for the next race meeting. In the early 1990's our totalisator agency board ran all the off-track betting in Australia. We were restricted to around 500 races per week across three codes. Now, that is nearly 4000 races per week. That is only the entrée to the thousands of other races that online bookmakers cover from other jurisdictions around the world. That just covers racing, and there are many times more markets covering the array of sports that are on every minute of the day. All of these are available from the marketplace that sits on everyone's smart phone. When it was a hobby, I looked forward a few days for the next race meeting but now there is never a break until you choose to take it. When you are an addict, making that choice is virtually impossible.

I sometimes wonder what would have happened to me if I had some form of scope to embezzle funds. While I was never close to considering bank robbery or any such form of crime to fund it, something more white collar may have been within my capabilities given the opportunity. I am glad it didn't. There were so many ways that this ruined my life, both for the impact on myself and the impact on my relationships with others. Ten times I've thought I've hit rock bottom but one way or another I kept going. I went 2 months without a bet but ended that with another binge. I then would go a few weeks without a bet before I felt the need to remind myself. The same pattern followed. An astute bet, a winner, a sudden belief that I'd changed before a gradual acceleration of bets giving back the winnings and a little more on top. With money in an account, however large or small, stopping is an overwhelming challenge. How someone can continue to do this to themselves given the indescribable self-loathing that follows a losing session is something I can't explain. Plenty of gamblers have been there once or twice and learnt a lesson. Addicts find that part of a normal day. We are every bit as fucked up as the worst heroin junkies, even worse in some respects as nobody can see the consequences. I sat at work after a binge and all anyone would think was "he looks tired." A drug addled employee wouldn't have been able to survive that experience without being clearly identified.

If anyone could hear the thoughts I had as I rode through here, they would think I was trying to pass the buck and blame society, gambling companies, Ash Wednesday, Olivia's death or Mr. Harris for my own weakness. That isn't what I think at all. Everything in life inter-relates, so this addiction does have part of its root in society, gambling companies and the tragedies through my life, but it doesn't mean I'm not responsible. I know I am, and it adds to the other factors of self-hatred. I hate that I can be so easily controlled.

I screwed up my lungs and my heart by smoking cigarettes, consumed by that addiction for 25 years. I screwed up my liver through an alcohol addiction that consumed me. I have destroyed my financial security by a gambling addiction. All of these have torn more seriously at my mental health and my feelings of self-worth. The blame for each of them was my own. The role of anyone or everyone else is comparatively inconsequential, but if as a society we want to improve outcomes we need to understand the full picture. We can jail gambling addicts for the crimes they commit, but surely a better solution is to stop the crimes and the addictions that fuel them first? I know which sounds like the choice of a progressive society.

The path bends fractionally by the shelter. From one day to the next it varies which subset of the group I see, but as I've christened them Maggie, Leo, Dave and Alby are all there this morning. No celebrity lookalikes, they feel more like prophets of my future than people from my past.

Leo and Dave are usually facing the opposite direction and have never taken up too much of my thoughts. Maggie is the most regular fixture. I can't tell if she is mid-thirties or mid-sixties, such is her haggard face, developed from years of hard living. Similarly, Alby is hard to pick, though certainly younger. He has a thick mane of lustrous hair that is his pride and joy. I sense the comb that is always in his hand is his most valuable possession. Often he is combing it as I pass in the morning. For someone who looks so dishevelled in every other way, this seems nonsensical. Through the addictions I've known, I understand it. In a life of complete disorder, having one element of total control and complete pride, carries a significance that most people can not understand.

As often is the case, Maggie is enjoying the exquisite pleasure of a cigarette. Not a full cigarette straight from the packet, but a crafted self-rolled combination of whatever unburnt tobacco she had found from butted out cigarettes on the streets over the previous day. Cigarettes rarely tasted that exquisite to me when I smoked, but I remember the feeling when the cravings were at their absolute strongest. The moment of lighting up and having that first drag was absolute heaven, and it is that moment that Maggie is getting to experience when I see her. When I pass through, only one of them is ever smoking. When resources are so scarce, everyone needs to bask in the smell as each other has their smoke before its time to switch roles. Most people wouldn't understand this but when you've lived it, you understand it.

I'm past them now but still thinking closely about their lives. In all likelihood I would join them one day if I lived long enough. I'm sure they see me and so many others pass them as we head from our warm homes to our comparatively lucrative jobs, and they envy us. I don't think I can say I envy them but on a day like today I think they have a better quality of life than me.

The less you have the more you appreciate the little that is yours. When I was at university, I had weeks where I had to live off $10. I would at times have just one bland meal a day but by God did I enjoy it. I had to ration my cigarettes and it was also the time that I loved smoking the most. This doesn't mean I am glad to be in my current financial position. I hate it. I hate that it comes from a point of addiction. I hate that I have so many restrictions on what I can and cannot do. I hate that every pay day begins a series of financial juggles as I seek to pay money of each of my debts. I hate that the following day begins a countdown of how many days remain before I get paid again, thinking that will be the day that I can treat myself. The reality always sets in that payday is actually just repayment day.

I always intended to one day buy a pouch of tobacco and leave it under this shelter for Maggie and Leo to find. They'd be too proud to feel good taking something they're offered, but finding something is a different thing altogether. They would feel like they'd had a spectacular windfall and would be happy for days. I remember having this thought on at least 100 previous mornings but haven't ever done it, so it remains nothing more than a good intention. Probably may help if I had the money to pay my own bills first.

I romanticise the good memories and then align them inappropriately. I remember the good times I've had on race-courses, with days of triumph that I will never forget. More often were the vast collection of nightmares that I never completely wake up from, where the results were vastly different. I tell myself that one day, maybe years from now I will be able to return to the way things were 20 years ago when I could study the racing guide, go to the track and enjoy my day to some extent, win, lose or draw. Maybe I could, but how much value would that add to my life anyway?

I have closed accounts and made it impossible to do it to myself any longer. It didn't stop the desire, but by eliminating the opportunity, I have gotten rid of the problem. Desperate enough to bet, I can still use cash and make the effort of going to a betting shop but at least this reduces the impulsiveness of the act.

I dwell at times on the money that's gone. It gutted me whenever I considered how much longer I would have to work in jobs I hated, to make up for the monetary loss. Despite this, the money was comparatively insignificant. Gambling destroyed me. It cost friendships and relationships. It took my self-esteem. I am so much poorer in every way as a result.

Each day Leo and Maggie are smiling when I see them. They don't see me smile. My life isn't better or worse than theirs it is merely the net result of all the experiences that have shaped it, just as their lives are. Good and bad. Right and wrong. I don't want to live the way they do, though who knows, they may possess a level of self-respect or at least self-acceptance that I don't have. They will be here tomorrow. I won't.

I bet most people can't understand. If a bookmaker would accept that bet, I would certainly take it. Most people would say that my addiction makes as much sense as taking money out of my wallet and setting it on fire. Effectively it is the same thing. What person could rationally do that? Rationale plays no role in any of this.

This is where I have done the digging. Being broke isn't as bad as some would imagine but being as full of self-hatred that this addiction has made me is where the real damage is done. It has almost followed a pathway where the darker times have got, the more willing I've been to dig deeper further from the light. I can't bear the thought of anyone seeing the real me.

CHAPTER 31

WEDNESDAY MARCH 3, 2021

I wonder if the man at reception was curious. Am I the only person to have ever booked a room here with this intention? This isn't my first time, so clearly it doesn't always play out as expected.

I almost pass this hotel on every morning on my commute. Just a little further west of where I cross South Terrace, it's an ideal spot for my needs. Reasonably priced, more than tall enough.

It was nearly 12 months ago that I came here the first time. I left work before the end of the day and just felt an overwhelming darkness. Walking home I saw this place and from nowhere felt compelled to take a course of action. When I got up to my room on the 9th floor I burst into tears and couldn't make sense of what option to take. I went out on the balcony only after a sense of calm had taken over me. As I leaned over the rail in what I'd envisaged would be a momentary pause before jumping, I knew that this was not the option for me at that time. I did however stare at the ground beneath and knew that I had certainty at my command. I could end things at the moment of my choice, and if the need became great enough, here was my ending point.

Back inside, I decided that if the day was getting closer, there was little to be lost by holding back from anything I could experience. I found a phone number in the newspaper and within the hour I had paid female company in my room. I had never hired a prostitute, never even contemplated doing so, yet in the whirlpool that my mind had become it didn't seem like a strange option to take. I couldn't be sure how long it had been since I had last had sex, but at least a couple of years. I hadn't consciously ever thought that I'd missed it, yet as the minutes passed waiting for her arrival, it seemed like I'd been alone far too long.

Once the time came my perspective changed somewhat. Crystal, as she called herself, was attractive and friendly, self-assured, experienced and forward enough to be able to read her customer. She would make the experience the best it could be. In truth, a manufactured sexual encounter with nothing more to it couldn't be satisfying. I went through the motions, not with any true pleasure, but the moment of orgasm was powerful. Not the physical sensation, but the vision in my head. I was falling through the sky. My mind had drawn parallels between what I used this room for and my intended use. However unfulfilling the sex was, it remained a vastly superior option to instant death. Based on the cost of the room and Crystal, I knew that I couldn't develop this into a habit every time the darkness became too much.

Moments after ejaculation I was already wanting her out of the room. I wanted to lay alone with my thoughts. For her, time was money, so I didn't have to wait long. I reflected on what would no doubt be a once only experience. No regrets, because that is the way I must live at this point, but equally no positivity to the memory.

I had a second visit here in January. That day was in the middle of a heatwave, and without working air-conditioning at home, I was motivated primarily by the need for a good nights sleep. I felt so physically and mentally drained from a lack of sleep which had combined with a major depressive episode to leave me completely lacking in desire to live. I wasn't intending to do anything final, but having the simple option there for me seemed like a reasonable plan B.

I'd had a relapse with my drinking at the time, which gave the evening a degree of inevitability. No doubt I would be spending some part of the evening hanging on to the railing of the balcony, looking over the edge with my head spinning at the sight of the ground below me and hearing voices calling me to join them. When the comfort of the cool air-conditioned room combined with my unimaginable fatigue and the quick consumption of several long glasses of vodka, I collapsed before the opportunity to do myself any real damage occurred. This time there was no waking up in a nightmare, and I slept for close to thirteen hours. Feeling better than I'd normally expect, I checked out and beat the heat on the four-block journey back to work.

Now things are different. I'm not here today for air-conditioning, for sleep or with an intention to be at work early tomorrow. I'm here because I can do it no more. Any of it. I no longer feel like I'm so deep in the pit that I just struggle to see the outside world. I feel unable to breathe, the pit filled in with dirt, burying me alive. There isn't an upside or an escape. I wake each morning disappointed to see a new day. I can only see two results to any moment; disappointment or nothing. Disappointment is my constant companion, while the only way I can meet nothing is with the ultimate finality. That is what I am here for.

There isn't one thing that tipped me over the edge. The cycle that started decades ago was possibly always destined to prompt my end. Any given time when too many triggers presented at once was likely to be the time it would happen. This week seems to be it.

I've tried of late; I really have. I've tried to re-establish contact with friends from the past, in order to rekindle joyful memories. I have dated for the first time in several years, to stave off my constant loneliness. I have put in so much extra effort at work, to avoid the inevitable conflicts. I've faced phobias in having medical checks done to allow peace of mind, though this has led to the revelation of a heart condition that, without major surgery, could kill me at any point. Primarily it is now three months since I have had a drink. I never expected the universe to repay my efforts with instant results, but I feel like I'm copping more slaps in the face than I can cope with right now. Some things I might be taking harder than they warrant, but I don't have the capacity to regulate my feelings. I react how I do because I'm human. I feel what I feel, not what I choose.

Last Wednesday I got the news that I would be moved to a different team at work. Not a big deal in the scheme of things, but at this stage it's had a big impact on me. I had instigated such positive change in my current area in the past few months, turning around substantial backlogs with more efficient process improvements. The results had started to shine through. Now I must begin again, with the painstaking process of instigating changes and doing so with unproductive people around me. The team leader who has failed in this role is moving into the role where I've ensured the hard stretch is now complete. I feel like I'm being punished for succeeding while she's rewarded for her failures. It shouldn't matter, but in my current state it is taking the last of my air.

Thursday, I came home to unwelcome news in the post with another attempt to refinance rejected. I am paying excessively high interest that sees me continuing to go backwards financially. I've made this mess but for all my efforts at repairing the damage, I constantly seem to fall further behind. I'm not seeking debts to be written off, just consolidated at a reasonable rate. Everybody wins, but I guess they don't appreciate anything as a win unless somebody is getting screwed as a result.

Friday I was reading the newspaper online and saw the feature story of a teacher convicted of child sex offences against two boys in the early 1980's. Sure enough, as I dug into the article there he was, Stuart Harris. He was remanded in custody awaiting sentencing. As much as this may seem like a reason to celebrate, my happiness was short lived. Yes, it felt great to know that bastards' evil had caught up to him, but as any survivor of sexual abuse knows, every time the event is brought back into your mind the horror replays. I had a weekend where I couldn't escape from visions of his face in my mind. All the negativity that he brought to my life was on constant replay. Knowing that he has been convicted is an objective met, but its therefore one less thing that I'm needed to keep going for.

Sunday, as challenging as it was destined to be, I decided to follow through on a date I had planned with a lady I'd met on-line named Chelsea. The weekend had left me far from being in the best place for this, but it also reminded me of the need I had for companionship. I didn't need to dazzle, just be myself. I turned up a few minutes early and dealt with the awkward-ness of sitting waiting for her, expecting it not to be too long. As the time passed, I got up and wandered thinking she may be in another part of the pub, and we'd miscommunicated. I didn't want to look overly anxious, so I waited until she was half an hour late before trying to call her, but the phone rang out. I kept trying but there was nothing. I'd been stood up and I felt humiliated. Could I be blamed for having my first drink in months. And a second. And continuing. I'm not sure how much I'd drunk by the time I left a voice message on her phone, but I know that whatever I said didn't leave room for an explanation.

Feeling my lowest I bought a bottle to take home. When I arrived I started seeking an adrenaline rush through a decent gambling win. After betting amounts starting at $20 I ended up dropping over $2,000 before I'd exceeded the limits on all of my accounts. Tremendously depressed, it was only eventu-ally passing out from the spirits that prevented another night without sleep.

Waking up this morning it was a great understatement to say I felt like shit. For so long this was a standard feeling. Now that it no longer so familiar, the impact is substantially more severe. My head was pounding as I got on the bike to ride to work. As sick as I felt, the commute served as a reminder of how much healing this part of the day always provided me. I still felt awful when I arrived, but not as bad as when I left home. To be fair, that wasn't saying much.

Being inside the building saw me deteriorate fast. It seemed typical that the day I arrived late was the same day that three of my staff had called in sick. The shit had also hit the fan with the media running a story on a mistake our department had made. I didn't have an instants peace all day, constantly in demand to be doing three different tasks in each moment. If I'd had the access to it, I would have been drinking again, but I no longer kept anything in the office and had no prospects of escaping for ten minutes. All day I felt like my head was getting worse. By mid-afternoon I could cope no more. I knew I'd be in shit for leaving early but I figured at that point it didn't matter. Nothing did. While Sam, Madeleine and Terry were in a meeting, I logged off and walked out the door. I didn't know where I was going just so long as I went.

As soon as I was outside, I found myself walking towards South Terrace. My mind was black, yet in amongst the darkness was a clarity leading me here. I booked a room for the night and came upstairs. I didn't stop to buy anything to drink on the way. I didn't want any later perceptions to indicate that there was any form of accident to what happened. Not everyone was going to understand, but I didn't want any confusion based around what had happened, merely why.

I always wondered why anyone would write a suicide note. There is nothing that can be said that will justify your actions to most people, but as I arrived here, I felt the need to write a few words. Possibly this was for me more than for those who would read it.

I'm Sorry

I don't know if this is a result of my weakness or if my weakness is a result of things beyond my control, but I can face life no longer. I apologise to those who I know will never consider this an acceptable way to end life, but the existence I now experience is no longer an acceptable way for me to continue.

Life delivers tragedy to everyone at some point, so I understand there will be many people who consider that I have over emphasised what I have endured. Maybe a better person would cope with what I have experienced. Sadly, I have lost that capacity.

I feel as though life has been a journey in one direction where numerous events have scarred me. With each scarring I have been more vulnerable to other events which have in turn scarred me more greatly. I lost my childhood when my best friends were killed. I lost my innocence when I was abused by a teacher. I lost my will to live when I lost my daughter. I lost my mind to the control of addiction. I have lost the people that matter, the passions that excited me and the hope that drove me. For all that I have lost, there is nothing I have found to compensate.

I couldn't be sorrier. I have strived for the past decade towards finding a new life, but I just slip further away. As much as it is the ultimate dread, when there is no value left to life there is little choice. It is not a choice of life and death, it is a choice of agony and relief. I have endured the agony for as long as I could. I now choose relief.

Before finishing I was interrupted by my phone. Cleo. What the hell could she want? She'd sent me a text asking if I was free now and could she phone me? I guess it made sense that she would be the last person I'd ever talk to. If there had ever been a point in my life when I felt I was normal and I belonged, it was within the time we were together. She may have taken the shovel to help dig my pit at the end of our relationship, but from the time we got together until Olivia died, it felt like we were making each others lives richer. Hindsight proved to me how unsuited we had been. We had made significant efforts to overcome our incompatibility, but what wasn't real could never really work long term. The memories hurt, but I had retained enough respect for her that I decided to call her.

Cleo told me that she'd just had a miscarriage a couple of weeks ago and she wasn't coping. She said that her partner had been no help and she didn't know who else to turn to.

'Even after all these years there's still never been anyone who can help me through crises like you,' she told me.

I don't think I said a word of any real assistance to her, but it had moved my mind so far from where it had been that I was healing myself. I wasn't sure if it was wise or not, but I told her where I was, the reason for being there and some of the precipitating factors.

'Fuck, Anthony. You cannot ever think that way. You mustn't ever. I don't minimise anything you've ever suffered but I promise you that you haven't done anywhere near as much as you've needed to in fighting the pain. Who have you talked to? How often? How in depth? You need serious counselling. Medication. Help. Do everything that a team of experts tells you for twelve months, then we can talk again about all you've done.'

We talked for more than four hours. She didn't make me feel better as such, but she did make me see a level of reason. There has been a part of me that has felt a level of bitterness towards her for over a decade. Like today, I hear from her maybe once a year when she has a problem and that's all. I realise that she can't be there for me when I need her, as I never come forward expressing that need. Like everyone else in my life, I never reach out. Relationships will always be one dimensional if you don't allow them to be anything else.

I spent nearly half an hour under a hot shower before laying in the comfort of the bed that was so much more inviting than what I sleep in at home. I read over the note I'd been writing before screwing it up and throwing it in the general direction of the bin. My mind was in so many separate places; the headache and drain of last night and the day at work was still with me but somewhat superseded by the emotional rollercoaster of the hours I'd spent in the room. I walked in here sure I would never leave, but now I felt like there was a pathway. I couldn't yet say I had reason or hope, but I had some form of direction. I was still buried deeply in my pit, but Cleo of all people had at least been able to direct a tiny fragment of light on me.

CHAPTER 32

8.46AM

I've reached South Terrace. From here I go straight across, but if I turned left and travelled west for a hundred metres, I'd be at that hotel again.

I've barely drank or gambled in the fourteen months since that night. The couple of times I have weakened, I've been reminded of my inability to maintain control over the habits. I never will be able to be a social drinker or gambler. When I do either, it's to deal with pain of some sort. I haven't found a better way of dealing with the pain, I have just learnt to have more acceptance of the role the pain has in my life.

The Two Dan's are walking along South Terrace as I wait for cars to pass before I cross into the square mile of the city. All the characters that define my ride to work have been out today and the flamboyance of Dan number one as he relays a story to his more discreet partner gets me out of the moment that was sinking me. On another day I would delve deeper into the soap opera of their lives as I see them. Today, they've enough competition for screen time that their role is more cameo in nature.

The Two Dan's confused me for quite some time. I saw them most days on my commute and wondered whether they were brothers or lovers. Of course, there is an enormous realm of options between these two, but they looked sufficiently similar that brothers was my initial thought. With time, their interactions seemed something more. They don't hold hands, yet they walk so closely together and look so engaged by each other's presence that in time I became convinced they were a couple. Realistically the truth of their relationship is irrelevant. They are real people, almost certainly named something different, but in my head exists only the alternate version I have created. In that version they will always be The Two Dan's. In the soap opera of my head, the plot keeps working around this mystery.

It is usually on the ride home when I see them at various points in this area. Both are always dressed in casual business attire like I wear to work. I can't quite work out where they would fit in my workplace. Whenever somebody else gets in an elevator with me, I play *"Guess which Floor"*. The IT people who work on level 7 are the ones I have the best success rate at picking. Doesn't matter how hard they attempt to blend in, there is something about them that screams out their career choice at first sight. The HR crew on level 3 and the accountants on level 5 usually stand out too. I think I'm a sufficiently experienced and skilled player at this game that few people trick me these days.

On the different route I take riding home, I often pass the Two Dans right by St Andrews Hospital, where my father passed away in 2013. Eighteen months after his granddaughter died, I was nowhere near ready for more loss.

My father was a great man in many ways, but one of his great failings was his inability to adapt. As life progressed it passed him by as he looked on at a world he struggled to keep up with. He seemed to get stuck in one point of life and everything paused at that moment. I couldn't even tell you the year, but everything from his hairstyle and clothes, his political views and attitudes towards social issues never changed in even the slightest way.

Dad was 45 when I was born and was quite a bit older than the fathers of any of my friends. While the difference may have been five to ten years, it seemed like a generation. He was closer in his stage of life, if not his age, to the grandparents of my friends. Even then, many people older than him were still less stuck in an era that had passed than what he was.

Now that I've reached that age, I understand the things I couldn't back then. There is no way I am as set in a time warp as he was, but I can see the romance and appeal that lies in by-gone eras. As much as some choose to put everything down as progress, I believe that progress is often a misused word for change. Change is often good, but not always. Even when change is predominantly good, it is rarely entirely good. The city I live in is better than it was when I was a child in many ways, but that hasn't come without costs. While some people ignore the costs, my father saw nothing else.

One of my mother's most effective methods of telling me off as a child was to use the phrase "*You're just like your father.*" Instantly this would have the impact of stopping whatever foolish act I was currently performing and behave more how she would like. Obviously I had worked out early enough that being just like my father was never a desired outcome. It took me several decades but eventually I realised that being like my father was far more ideal than I could have ever believed.

I remember the night that Mum told him she was leaving him. I was in the lounge room watching the Seoul Olympics. However Dad had taken the news, when I saw him, the first thing he did was ask me the score in the hockey game. He displayed no real emotion, though in hindsight, I know he would have felt broken. That was his way. Even though I saw him fight it a couple of times near the end, he never cried in front of me. He never expressed emotion to me. That's not entirely true, for I often saw tears of joy. He wouldn't hide his emotions watching a film or cheering his football team, but anything truly personal was off limits. That would be dealt with where nobody could see. No doubt there would have been some instances where he'd share some of this with Mum and in later years his partner Joan, but even they would have been sheltered from most of his emotions. Is there any surprise the same is true of me?

Dad was born during the Great Depression and had a very tough upbringing. His father never wanted children and the scarcity of resources in the era further validated this wish. Feeding an extra mouth was more trouble than he thought it worth. The family had a small vegetable farm, fifty miles south of Adelaide, but it was barely self-sufficient. At twelve, Dad was taken out of school and sent to work as an apprentice in a furniture factory. It is incomprehensible to me how a pre-teen could spend twelve hours a day away from home doing hard labour for unimaginably small wages, for his parents and him to survive. He did it though. He worked hard. He learnt. He strived.

Dad ended up with a successful business despite lacking any form of formal business training. He was self-taught on most issues of management, marketing, and compliance. He wrote skilful eye-catching advertisements. He did his own book-keeping, using his own methodologies. With every day he learnt more about the lines between success and failure in his field, and he became an authority.

As a child, Dad's home life was traditional of the era. His mother did all the cooking. At the end of his apprenticeship, he moved to the city and boarded with an old lady who took on the same role. He didn't move from that environment until after his wedding when Mum became the newest person to cook his meals and wash his clothes. Twenty years later, when Mum, Tim and Vanessa had all gone, it was just him and me. We developed a new food preparation plan. Every week we rotated between the meals we were capable of organising; take-away Chinese, take-away Hamburgers, take-away Pizza, take-away Greek, take-away Fish and Chips, take-away Chicken and the great variety that came with a counter meal at the local pub. That was complimented by lunches from the school-tuck shop that covered the choice of either a pasty or a sausage roll. Either option would be accompanied by similar variety, with either a chocolate or cinnamon donut to complete my lunch. The only real change in my diet came when visiting Mum in Brisbane for school holidays.

While some people may have been appalled at the way we lived, my memories of it are wonderful. When he met Joan, he again had a woman who cooked for him. They lived separately but he ate dinner at her place each night while I began cooking for myself. His failings in the kitchen spurred me to learn and helped my independence. I developed a love for cooking that stayed with me throughout life. I regret not pursuing it as a career. Without the way I began, I suspect I never would have been so passionate about food. I still recall the idyllic way that the bonds between Dad and me grew so strong in that period of time and I savour those memories fondly.

I look a lot like my father did at my age. When I last lived with him, I'd answer the phone and people were convinced it was him, such was the similarity of our voices. We had similar senses of humour, personalities, and interests. Like him I've always been shy in new surrounds while being extraverted once comfortable in groups. I have seen the similarities between us for as long as I've been willing to acknowledge the truth. Annoying habits that I always considered to identify in him and not notice in me were more circumstantial in nature than they were true pictures. Dad had incredibly strong attributes, and although I haven't always flourished in revealing them, I know I carry many of these. I'm far more practiced in the vast array of character flaws that Dad occasionally also revealed.

I wonder if life had ever been as black for him as it has been for me. Once he tiptoed around the topic of suicide when it had come up in the media. Like always he was reluctant to share anything too emotional, but there was enough to suggest a level of understanding of those who have done this, or attempted. He never went further with me to give me any real certainty of what he'd experienced. If he looked down on me when I was in the hotel room close to the end could he have understood? Had he been there? Is it just another example of me having been just like my father?

CHAPTER 33

Across South Terrace the final change of scenery is apparent as I'm now in the city itself. The little backstreets in the southern part of Adelaide's central business district are a real mix of old-style houses and redeveloped inner-city apartments. The apartments are mainly an average impression of the equivalent developments in bigger cities. They do nothing for the character of the city. I love some of the small houses that shine a light on the city of a century ago, but they seem to be getting dominated more each year. Some level of development seems to have occurred everywhere. The houses that remain are either heritage protected or are a development waiting to happen. Unfortunately, heritage protection is of only so much value. The cultural positive that these houses provide loses quite a bit when they are surrounded by 21st century development.

My route takes me along quiet Charlotte Street and I always get a bit of a laugh to myself as I pass Don Lane, a tiny offshoot that is disproportionate to the late television entertainer of the same name. Across the next main block, I pass

209

a short walkway until reaching a one-way side street where I turn left. Another identity appears, Margot Kidder, dubbed after the actress who played Lois Lane. She has a small dog she takes for a walk each morning and I can usually set my watch to her. Her husband George Reeves, named after the actor who played Superman is sometimes with her.

What should be, and usually is, a quiet peaceful street seems far from it today. An elderly couple live immediately adjacent to George and Margot's house. I often see her out the front having a cup of tea on the veranda. Sometimes I see her out here waving goodbye to her husband as I ride past. I've never given either of them names. For some reason nothing has ever come into my mind. '*Old married couple from Wakenham Street*' didn't have much of a flow to it, but nothing else stood out to give them.

Today they shape like two different people to what I'm used to seeing. The man is screaming at his wife by the front door. Even at my gentle speed I am past the commotion quickly enough that I didn't get any real insight into what the issue was, but the ferocity of the argument had me feeling very uneasy. What can a passer-by do anyway? When something happens on the street, you can see exactly what the situation is and whether getting involved is appropriate. Inside the front door of a strangers home is a different scenario altogether. I know the people in the sense of familiarity by sight, but I don't truly know them. Is this normal for them? Is the man a nutcase? Is the woman in any sort of physical danger? I momentarily considered riding back and asking Margot Kidder if this is normal, but I think she'll be more freaked out by me and my familiarity than by what is happening in her neighbours house. She isn't Margot, she is a stranger, as much as I forget at times.

I continue. As I've turned back, I can see that the husband has started walking down the street. He may not get the normal wave goodbye this morning, but hopefully absence will calm the situation.

Having just thought so much of my father and his up-bringing, his parents now come to mind. Grandpa died before I was a year old, so I have no recollection of him at all. Grandma survived long enough for me to remember her much more. All the recollections I have are of someone who only spoke when spoken to. She did as she was told, and in my time, with Grandpa no longer around, there was nobody to tell her what to do. The impact of this was a life of sitting in a chair waiting. Waiting for nothing, but waiting, nevertheless.

I've never heard any suggestion that she was hit, but she had a set of scars from what she did receive from him. He made every decision. He set the rules and she should never dare think that she was an equal partner in the marriage. She gave birth, but that wasn't a good thing. Grandpa never wanted children, so the accident that was Dad didn't earn Grandma respect, just anger.

I will never know how accurate it is, but the picture I have of grandpa in my head resembles the man at number 8. The screams at a placid wife. A woman who is quite befitting of the memory of my grandma. A woman who suffered so much and received so little. A woman who was dominated in a time when society considered that acceptable. A woman who only got the freedom to live so late in life that she was unprepared to know how to do so. Every visit to her house was punctuated by large gaps of silence where everyone tried to produce something to say. Her replies would always be limited to *"yes," "that's nice"* or something similar.

For so many fathers, the lessons they source for this role lie in their own upbringing. Dad's role model in fatherhood had done such an ordinary job that he knew the best approach was to be the complete opposite, but there were limits within him that he never overcame. There would never have been a limit to what he would do for me, his generosity and his patience, but anything that involved revealing too much of the person within remained hidden. He seemed a simple man, and it's only been through my own journeys that I've begun to identify the additional complexities that made him who he was.

Sometimes opposites are far closer than they seem at first. Love and hate couldn't seem more opposite, yet the passion of each can lead to the same results. Olivia as my purist love, and Stuart as my greatest hate were the two people in life who most led me to my current state of mind. I learnt fatherhood by following the example of my father. He learnt fatherhood by following the opposite to the example of his father. Both of us ended up at the same place from these opposite roads.

Maybe it's the product of what I am that makes me say it, but so what if someone destroys themselves. Not that their actions won't have some impact on those around them, but its negligible compared with what abusive men do. Destroying the lives of those you claim to love. Do they even claim this? Dad was never shown anything indicating love from his father and I'm sure grandma wasn't either. That said, when he married Grandma, he stood in a church and made vows to say he did and he would.

I can never remember my grandma without thinking of her as a victim. Now I could never see this woman from number 8, without thinking the same of her. While my disdain for the man is great, I now also feel a sense of anger at myself. Circumstances may not have been suitable for me getting involved in a strangers fight, but that is something where each person draws their own line. I feel as though I have a set of ideals that tell me to jump in and defend victims but it's in constant competition with the other voice in my head telling me to stay out of strangers lives.

After seeing them so many times, it is on my last day passing their house that I finally have names for them. Grandma and Grandpa may sound like the standard nicknames to give people of their ages, but in this case it has a particular relevance.

When your mind is dominated by contradictions you can't avoid the fact that one voice in your head gets chosen while another gets ignored. It seems like in every instant I always resort to ignoring the voice that promotes what is right in favour of the voice that encourages what is easy.

Calling them easy options is such a misnomer. It may avoid the harder challenge in the moment but if it leaves you dwelling long enough on what you didn't do, you've hardly bought a better result. All I do is dwell, and now this old couple will be another example of a so-called easy choice that haunts me.

CHAPTER 34

SATURDAY AUGUST 28, 1993

The last bus home leaves from outside the railway station at 11.45pm. Miss that and there isn't any sort of alternative for me. I haven't got any money for a taxi. and there is no chance of me risking my life by walking home through the parklands. It may not really be so dangerous, but they're not the kind of chances I like taking. Plus, I'm not walking four kilometres at this time of the night. Any time, come to think of it.

Griffin and I spent most of the evening in the games arcade where Sean works. We spent a few bucks, but Sean always looks out for us, and he was able to give us some free games. We'd had a decent night without costing much. Griffin's bus wasn't due until right on midnight from Currie Street, so he was still there when I left.

I smoked my last cigarette while I walk to the station. I wished I had more than one on me as I knew I'd want to have one while I walked home from the bus stop at the other end. I must admit I'm not much good at rationing things. I always end up regretting having no money, no cigarettes or whatever else it may be after blowing what I've got straight away. It's actually pretty good that I've held on to this one last cigarette.

It's only about 11.35 as I get to North Terrace, directly opposite the stop where my bus departs. Impatience isn't my issue, although I can't say I enjoy sitting waiting at bus stops for extended periods, but my main concern is that the railway station area isn't always the safest. Getting the bus home from here after school is never a problem, but by late evening it's not such a good place to be. While I'm waiting to cross the road at the lights, I try and survey the scene as best as I can. It appears that none of the rumoured gangs that supposedly frequent the area were present and I would be safe in the well-lit area by the bus stop. The only real alternative I had was to walk up a stop and there seemed to be just as much likelihood of running into trouble doing that.

There are two park bench style seats at the bus stop, though more people seem to stand back against the wall of the train station. During the week, the benches are the domain of people much older than me, so I allow my tired self the pleasure of the seat now. The time drags slowly which tends to happen when you check your watch each minute.

There would have been no more than two or three minutes left to wait when a guy sat down next to me and another one stood in front of me. They were probably a couple of years older than me, and their appearance didn't have me wasting time wondering if I needed to worry. I did! The one standing in front of me ensured that I wasn't going to move. The only question was, what did they want. If robbery was their motivation they weren't going to be getting much out of me. Possibly this was just their way of passing the time.

The guy sitting next to me saw my cigarette lighter sticking out of my pocket.

'Give us a smoke.'

'I had my last one walking down here. Haven't got any man, sorry.'

As I finished saying that a fist made heavy contact with my face. I've been pushed around once or twice in my life, but never punched. More than any pain I felt, shock was the primary impact. Not that I necessarily should have been shocked, as I thought something like that was on the cards as soon as they turned up, but I didn't see it coming at that moment.

'Oi what did you do that for,' the seated guy said to his friend. Although that implied empathy he was laughing as he said it, as was the guy who hit me. 'We can figure out something else for him if he ain't gonna give us a smoke.'

I quickly shot a look to the side and saw a group of about ten guys not more than twenty metres away. I was sure they were connected to these two, and if I tried to jump and run, they'd have me covered. I offered my lighter as it was the only thing I had of any value.

'Not much use without a smoke to light is it,' he said. 'Give us money then.'

'I haven't got any,' I said nervously.

'Bullshit.' The guy in front hit me again, while the guy who had been sitting next to me used the lighter to set fire to my hair. As I used my jumper to try and put this out, others from the group had run over towards me. I was kicked and punched again, and with me on the ground bloodied, burned and petrified, they sought to go through my pockets and take anything they could. They took my keys, the relatively cheap watch I wore and an empty wallet, but as I'd said, there was no money.

It was all over in seconds. I think there were people yelling to try and create a diversion, but it was too much of a blur for me to really know. Nobody dared to confront the group, but within a minute of things escalating, they'd fled, making sure they were long gone before the inevitable arrival of the police.

A guy of about 50 was the first person who came over to me.

'I thought you were one of them' he said to me. 'If I'd realised I would have come over and helped you.'

My prominent blonde locks couldn't have contrasted more with the group so I don't know how anyone could have seen the event without knowing exactly what went on. I think Goliath, as I called him, seemed big enough to have been capable of taking the whole gang on. It seemed more likely that he wanted to be able to present himself as good intentioned, though he really never wanted to take a chance.

The bus then pulled up and opened its doors. I didn't know what to do. Goliath had said someone had called the police and an ambulance which I didn't feel I needed.

'I'm meant to catch this bus,' I said, struggling to even get myself sitting upright.

'Na you've got to make those black shits pay. Wait for the cops. Plus, you'll need some medical attention.'

Goliath seemed to be a more dangerous person than the guys who had attacked me. While he'd indicated he would have been a hero, he did nothing other than show his racist attitudes. He was the type to look for any opportunity to feel even bigger than he literally is. The people who attacked me were arseholes. No stereotyping or racial profiling was needed. They were all male, but he didn't stereotype based on gender. They were all teenagers, but he didn't stereotype on age. Race was the only basis of his stereotyping. I was going to wait, but I was more comfortable with him getting on the bus and leaving the scene.

The police came shortly before the paramedics who attended to my facial wounds and told me I'd need to go to the hospital for x-rays. I had been kicked in the chest hard and they suspected I may have damage to my ribs. The police investigation was short. One of the officers seemed to have taken his queues from Goliath. Neither of them had enough questions to persist for long. They knew the gang. They expected a call like this at some stage through the night. I was just the member of the public who'd drawn the short straw.

'If you'd been in a less public area it probably would have been a lot worse. The noise and attention would have helped keep their priority on getting out of here quickly,' the younger cop said.

'Probably a good thing nobody tried getting involved,' his colleague said, explaining that such interruptions often led to more force being used. 'The guys lurking back would have been armed. If there were more people to deal with, that's when they step in and it gets dangerous fast.'

'You're lucky they lit your hair first when you were able to stop it. Burns could have really made it something terrifying,' the first officer added.

I didn't need to know about burns. Since the age of four, I have been all too aware of the threat of fire.

I also knew too much of the perils that can exist in these scenarios. Ricky, a guy my sister had worked with a few years earlier, had recently been killed in Sydney. He had stepped into a confrontation where two men were attacking a woman. They turned on him, stabbing him multiple times. Even with this interruption, the woman still didn't escape them. His heroism not only proved fatal, but also in vain.

Sometimes dreadful things happen. Some of them are catastrophic. Tonight's could have been, but fortunately it will serve more as a lesson for the long term. I might feel sore for a few days, but in the scheme of things, all will be alright.

I was pissed off that Goliath, for all his words, took no action. It didn't need to be physically confronting the attackers, but making some noise, telling them that the police were on their way, may have been enough to stop the trouble far earlier and less painfully. You're not a hero by making big statements, offensive or not. Heroism comes with actions, not words. It doesn't need to be physically taking on anyone, just anything that helps alleviate the problem. He chose to do nothing, which is understandable, but it takes away your right to talk so big at the end of the event.

If I was standing back and someone vulnerable had been sitting on the bench what would I have done? Not even worth asking, I know I would have done nothing. I also would have felt like a useless piece of shit as a result. Sometimes we need to know our place, even when we don't like that place. Life is not about winning every battle. Some battles we cannot win, and the aim is to escape while losing as little as possible.

CHAPTER 35

8.49AM

Some battles we cannot win, and the aim should be to lose as little as possible. Terry refuses to ever settle for less than victory, and usually fights to the death. I'm not a combative person and seek to avoid issues whenever possible. Once someone else starts a verbal joust, if I don't walk away fast enough, I don't walk away at all. My form of defence then becomes attack. In a test of minds, I have Terry beaten, but the battle is more complicated than that. There is no independent arbiter to analyse the arguments made. He will always maintain that he is right, and I am wrong, and with more logic and reason behind me, I will do the same. Nobody truly wins.

Friday's argument stemmed from a story about what I'd said in a private conversation. Giving benefit of the doubt, I could perhaps say that it wasn't *made up*, but a misunderstanding. This type of Chinese whispers is far too typical in the branch. It seemed like a kindergarten at times, with one desperate child running to the teacher to create trouble. This was easily done as it was usually a fourth hand version of a story, changed at every step on the way. Some of these changes were innocent mistakes, but several people worked with motives.

The real origin stemmed back a couple of months earlier. I was chatting with Brooke at the other end of the floor. She'd been told she was moving to the branch's call centre in the following fortnight. I made some comments about the area she was moving to, and how it wasn't being managed as it should be. We were good friends, so it didn't seem inappropriate to share our views. What made it not so appropriate were the ears popping up at the adjacent desk. A new employee who I didn't know, named Rachel. I'd said that the management wasn't running the Call Centre appropriately, but at least I didn't name anyone, and this new girl wouldn't know the people down there anyway.

So much for that. Rachel had been hired and inducted by Terry. He quite liked the attractive young blonde, and she had clearly learnt that it was best to stay on his good side. Unbeknown to me, she detoured past his office every day before she left, popped in and mentioned anything she thought he would be interested in. Apparently that day, my conversation with Brooke was an example. That may be understandable, but she added more than a little sugar on top, and what Terry heard was something far more hostile than anything I had said.

'How dare you undermine other managers in front of new staff,' Sam yelled after summoning me to her office.

'I never did,' I replied.

'You were heard telling Brooke that Terry was incompetent in his management of the Call Centre.'

'That is completely untrue.'

'You never had that conversation?'

'I had a conversation with Brooke. I never mentioned Terry. I never said anyone was incompetent. I made the points that I have made since managing the Call Centre myself. A few slight changes could make it work better for the organisation, the clients and the staff. It was as much an attack on myself as it was on Terry, or you, or anyone else. I said it then, I will say it now to you and to anyone who cares to listen. I didn't denigrate any person, the organisation or the management.'

'It doesn't sound like you were being positive,' she said, a little calmer than she'd started. 'You are a part of the leadership of this branch. People listen to you, so you need to be seen to be supportive of the direction we are going.'

'Given how you started this chat, it seems like the word of a temp who has been here three weeks gets treated as gospel, while the words of a seven-year employee aren't considered sufficiently important to seek out before firing retributions. Isn't support a two-way street?' I could deal with copping my share when it was warranted, and in my case that was often enough. I wasn't willing to pay the price for what I had not done. She apologised if I had interpreted that way, but refused to acknowledge that this was how it had been meant.

'I was showing how I felt about team leaders using their influence. I wasn't suggesting that you'd done wrong,' she said defensively. However obvious a wrong doing was, there was always a reason or excuse to explain it. Like the word sorry, it only left her lips with a clarification. Her apologies were never for her actions, but for others interpretation of them.

I spoke to Brooke soon after, this time without the imaginative ears of Rachel nearby.

'She wants a permanent job. Figures her best way forward is to get the most senior person possible on side and fighting in her corner, so she tells him what he wants to hear,' Brooke later explained.

'I don't think Terry's opinion carries any weight with the rest of the management team,' I said. 'She's more likely to alienate herself riding his coat tails.'

'But she wouldn't know that. She knows Terry is higher up the chain than you and would therefore think that it makes that the right side to be on.'

Friday's fight with Terry emanated from the same type of scenario. Reporting from Rachel, though this time more fanciful. She had not been within earshot. We never mentioned the workplace at all. Complete fabrication in her quest for attention, yet again it had been treated as though it was a word for word account.

As I rode home on Friday night, the conversation with Terry replayed through my head, interspersing with what I expected from this mornings meeting with Sam. I had more difficulty dealing with the internal monologue when I was on my own than I had fighting Sam or Terry. At least a fight with them, however painful, would have an end. When it was just me, the conversation would repeat and circulate, never providing me an opportunity to stop and switch off.

The impact that this has on my health is significant. I thought I was too young to be worrying about such things. In my mind I am mid-twenties. In reality, I could have a child that age. I am not the young man I think, and my body has started to send me more of the hints to ensure I do not forget.

CHAPTER 36

8.51AM

Making my final left turn, I can now see the building straight ahead. I feel a sense of relief that I am close to the end of my ride. It is far from an exhausting journey, though more tiring than it used to be. At the end of last year I had major heart surgery. The recovery has been slow and painful. I had nearly three months off work and it was an additional month before I was back riding in. I was now managing the ride comfortably enough, but it still was not with quite the ease of years gone by.

Heart surgery has impacts far beyond what people may expect. Any major surgery has a pronounced physical effect on the patient, but there is a strong precedence for heart surgery patients to experience substantial mental health issues after the event. My general practitioner had mentioned that in the aftermath of such surgery a considerable number of patients developed suicidal thoughts, regretting the procedure. For someone like me, this was likely to be a risk. I reasoned that I was a dead man without the surgery, so I just had to accept the risks and do it.

If my body did not give me reminders, then they were guaranteed to surface each time I came to work, passing the hospital on the way. Sometimes I even see my surgeon on his way in or out of the building. The scar down my chest will be a permanent reminder, though not the only one. The surgery itself went smoothly, or so I was told, but the list of complications from after that date was extensive and the mental toll was as great as I had feared.

I was initially diagnosed with my heart issue nearly two years earlier. It was incredibly confronting to hear that I was on limited time. It did not feel like there was any choice to make; I may not be in love with life but living with the eternal question of which day it would be that my heart valve would burst and kill me was not a fate I looked forward to. The only logical option was to have the operation.

When I first saw a surgeon, he was quick to tell me that he was against doing the operation in the short term. The particular surgery was very high risk and while it would be essential in time, it was best to wait allowing me to live as well as possible in the meantime. Live well? Hardly.

'There is a three percent chance you'll die in surgery. There is perhaps a one in ten thousand chance you're valve will burst today and kill you. Every day those chances will increase by the smallest fraction, but by monitoring the valve over the next twelve months or so, we can gauge when the risk of doing nothing becomes greater than the risk of operating.' Dr Clifton was renowned as the best surgeon available. His calm calculations about my mortality were not the most reassuring thing to think about, but the reality of this field of medicine is that you're always best served with someone that astute and unemotional about their work.

It ended up nearly eighteen months on from the original diagnosis before we were ready to take the step. I do not know whether I was looking at this more as eighteen months of extra life experiences gained or eighteen months more of fear and trepidation allowed to fester. I certainly found my fears growing with time and in the month between the date being set and my admission date, I really began to accept that this could be the end of me. As I became more certain of this, I simultaneously became less concerned. Surely a failure to wake up would not be the worst way to go. I did not feel like there was enough that I really wanted to be surviving for. Whatever was to come, I felt ready.

Historically I have always suffered from serious anxiety around any form of medical procedure. I only needed to hear what was going to happen to be in trouble. Years ago I went into hospital to have my wisdom teeth removed. I had the procedure explained to me on admission and was then told to change into a hospital gown. Moments later they heard a crash; the words of the nurse were in my head as I got changed and I passed out at the thought alone. It's not the only time something like that has happened. While simple blood tests have never quite seen me pass out, I usually am on the way each time I have one. How was I now going to cope with open-heart surgery?

Being wheeled into the operating theatre I thought to myself how much calmer I felt than in far less threatening situations before it. I was about to be put to sleep and there was a three percent chance I would never wake up. I didn't care. There could be far more horrific fates, but I had spent so much time contenting myself with the prospect of quick and painless death that I chose not to think of anything more. The anaesthetists had trouble in the initial stage getting a line into my dehydrated body, but eventually success was found and without warning, I was asleep. My final memory was the anaesthetist's assistant mentioning that his name was also Anthony. I started to respond but do not recall finishing.

It had been soon after midday when they took me to theatre, and it was not until the next morning when I remember anything else. The operation itself was about four hours and although I am told that I did wake up the previous evening, I was in a far too drug-addled state to remember anything about it. The next morning, I was a little more conscious and aware of the pain more than anything else.

I remained in hospital for just over a week; roughly forty-eight hours in intensive care before spending the next five days in the cardiac ward. While this wasn't much different to the original expectations, it came only after a couple of occasions where it was suggested I'd be going home the next day if no complications arose. Complications certainly did arise, starting with a suspected stroke.

The hospital almost felt like a hotel. Modern and comfortable, laying in my bed in a spacious room of my own, I marvelled at how I was being treated better for the time I was in here than I ever could be outside. Three reasonable meals a day, not that they were overly appetising, meant that I was getting better nourishment than I did on the outside. I had a constant supply of effective painkillers that meant I felt sore rather than agonised. I had daily visits from my mother and sister who had come from Brisbane and Tasmania respectively, the first I had seen of either of them in four years. My mum would stay for an additional few days in line with the requirement that I had someone stay with me when I returned home. What someone of her age could possibly do me for was not explained, but in those situations, they believe that there needs to be someone who can at least call an ambulance for the susceptible person. I was not certain which of us they considered the more susceptible.

Every day the pain seemed a little better and the reliance on medication reduced fractionally. I was up walking the day I returned to the ward, albeit with the aid of a frame. I was encouraged to spend more time sitting up rather than laying down. Once or twice a day I was encouraged to walk a lap of the ward, and it took no time to graduate from a slow walk accompanied by the physiotherapist to confidently strolling the hallways on my own with no support necessary. I had a minor viral infection which they insisted needed fighting with drugs best supplied intravenously and that is what was keeping me inside. I was grateful it did.

Prior to the surgery I faced a condition that guaranteed my death in the next few years. After the success of the operation, there was no reason to indicate premature death was at all likely, so understanding the impact on depression is difficult. The operation itself was in no way the cause, but it is the reality of the way the average mind works that the change in circumstance that seemed positive when just a theory has a far more negative impact when it is put into practice. It is common enough that the term cardiac depression is extensively used for these situations.

Within days of returning home things started mounting up. The pain was remaining constant, and as much as the initial seven to ten days post operation had seen strong and steady improvement, progress decelerated quickly from that point. Given my doctors had provided me less pain relief for my return home than I had been accustomed to whilst in hospital, I was suffering more with time, not less. It was only a small part of the mental challenge, but a part that seemed unnecessary, given the ease there would be to prescribe appropriate pain relief. Considering my addictive nature, this might not be a mistake.

What people find most confronting is the underlying thought process that dominates the mindset of the depressed person post-operation. Far from relief to have overcome the traumas of the operation, it is almost a feeling of disappointment. I did not want to die under the knife, but there was a sense that it did offer me the potential of an easy escape from a life I'd had enough of. The ongoing threat of death from my heart had grown for two years and was all set for its pinnacle with the operation. Surviving this had left me with the downbeat reality that life just continues. The irrationality of the mind sets in; I did not want to die but I am not happy to be alive.

Depression is always a spiral and it proved exactly that way after the operation. Feeling worse I sort refuge through sleep increasingly. Spending more time in bed gave me less energy and reduced my appetite which then continued to leave me more fatigued and the cycle progressing accordingly.

I became more irritable. I lost enthusiasm for things, even simple pleasures such as reading or watching television. Each day there was less reason to be waking up and facing another day where there was nothing to look forward to, nothing to achieve and nothing more than the prospect of a return to bed.

Hopelessness was not new to me. I had been through enough episodes from my mid-teens onwards to understand the signs, but understanding was never an automatic precursor to resolution. Now I was at a point where I had the same miserable existence in front of me but with the added factors at play of a lifelong dependence on medication that would now be a part of every day. I had the sound and feel of a new heart valve that had such a disconcerting impact with every heartbeat that I could not feel relaxed with silence around me.

I regretted having had the operation. Why extend life expectancy if the term of one's life is depressing? Maybe it is a trick of the mind and I'd have been going more insane in the uncertainty that existed with my previous condition. Maybe I was doomed to feel this kind of way irrespective of what action I had chosen.

Coming back to work after ten weeks was a culture shock of its own. I have dreaded the workplace for as long as I can remember yet in the days building up to my return I was actually quite looking forward to it. The meaningless nature of my job didn't seem to matter once it gave me some small reason for getting out of bed. I knew it was not a feeling that would last. If nothing else it could serve as a signpost pointing me towards what I really needed to find in life. Like most people, I had to find a more genuine motivation going forward. A job, a career, a passion. Something that would not fade with familiarity. Maybe everyone sees the brightness fade after the beginning but not always to the same degree. I have known enough people who continue to find inspiration. Is it what they have found in their life or is it something deeper within them that allows them to find more in any given situation than what someone like me ever can? I have to believe there may be more available or how do I keep on going?

Work and the ride in is now as familiar as it was before the operation. The scar still serves as a reminder and I can still feel a small difference through my chest at times on the commute. The feeling of my more pronounced heartbeat ensures that I never push too hard to make a set of lights now. I'm encouraged to work my heart but what person can really feel comfortable pushing part of their body when they get such different signals pushing back at them. It may be perfectly healthy to have this feeling, but its not familiar enough to accept that at this stage.

As life has returned to normal, my feelings about all I went through have become less clear cut. Regret isn't the word to use, for I find it hard to argue against the actions I took. There was one viable option and I chose it. It wasn't an option that didn't carry its own set of negatives. I've experienced them all and know well enough that they were unavoidable. The medical professionals never really covered these issues, but I wasn't naïve enough to be unaware of what was coming. What goes up comes down, and in my case, far quicker and far harder.

The small focus that was directed towards my mental health seemed like one of the greatest examples of lip-service I had ever seen. They provided so much advice of what to do to assist my mental health, emphasising diet, exercise and focusing on the positives. Perhaps if I hadn't been so depressed I'd have been capable of doing these things, but given the situation it would have been similarly useful to suggest I just win the lottery.

Once I'm in the central business district I only have one set of traffic lights to deal with and sure enough I've just missed the green. Here with my building in full sight it I can always feel the windows like eyes upon me, staring and calling me in. Traffic barely moves on Pulteney Street heading north as peak hour bares its teeth and there's something reassuring that when I step inside I will be part of more order than I could hope for out here.

What does it matter that I missed the lights by a few seconds? Who knows, but what if Anne O'Connor had missed an extra set of lights on that fateful journey in 1984? Would the accident have happened? Every second, so many things happen that have some tiny impact. They can appear insignificant, yet somehow it can change the course of life for someone. Maybe there's been a point where I missed a set of lights that saved me from an accident. Nobody can ever know what would have happened if we'd been a moment earlier or later. When catastrophe happens, it is hard to avoid all the *if only* contemplations.

Maybe luck is everything. We all fall into the belief that our lives will be defined by doing the right things, working hard, being good to others but it may be a load of shit. Life may truly be defined by stepping out the door a moment earlier. Just catch that set of lights and get splattered by a truck. Be one person earlier to buy that lotto ticket and be set for life. A split second decision of whether to go to a function or not can be the difference in meeting that someone special – shit if

I didn't go to Jenny's engagement party would I have ever got to know Cleo? Would Olivia ever have been born? Would I have met someone else and had a child who lived and grew up safely and soundly? It's not just the person immediately impacted by these chance moments as everything flows through everyone connected. There is no limit to how different the world ends up through every fateful instant.

For someone who was always filled with dread on the way to work, it defies logic how much I put myself through on my morning rides. The part of the day that should relax me sometimes has the opposite effect due to my overactive mind. I'd like to say the day can only get better, but today that is not true.

CHAPTER 37

8.53am

I still must run up five flights of stairs before I clock-in. Run is hardly the right word, but as part of my ongoing rehabilitation, I have made it a routine to take the stairs each morning. The need to rehabilitate may no longer exist, but routines don't need a reason. When its automatic, it takes more thought to change than to continue, even if would be easier.

I'm meant to feel fresh and ready to face a daunting day of work, yet I feel drained. The passing of time has been a contradiction; it seems like only five minutes ago I was leaving home, yet I have virtually gone through my entire life in my head during that time. As years have passed, the familiarity of the workplace has made the days feel progressively longer and slower. I feel it killing me more each day I come here but the challenges of finding another option got greater with time.

My place in this building is the result of all the steps in my life, both those of my own volition and those forced upon me. I achieve nothing. I don't excel. I am a tiny cog in a wheel that could be easily replaced by another anonymous number.

To be fair, I do my job well and set a good example. At best, I can say that I provide some advanced level of guidance and development to some of the younger staff who may in time go on to make a more significant contribution. By any measure, none of this adds up to even a small percentage of what I am capable of, but it is something that I did once feel a sense of pride in. Diminished by those above me enough, this is just another place I don't belong. Sadly, the steps through my life left me too far away from the halls I should be walking at this time of my life.

Some people might think I'm refusing to take responsibility for my failings, but that isn't true. Decades of self-loathing don't come from shedding all blame. My failures are my own. I accept full responsibility for all of them. Reasons and excuses are very different. I blame myself appropriately but I also understand that other people would have ended in other places even making the choices I made. Nobody ends up where they do purely by the choices they make. There are factors beyond our control that impact where we are. The traumas through childhood didn't seal my fate but they were the beginning of the pit being dug for me. Each extra step of my descent has come at least in part because of the first one.

Out in the corridor of the sixth floor, I don't see a soul when I arrive. Good. The last thing I need at this point is to be delayed in social niceties. I feel hypocritical saying this; one of my main frustrations with our workplace is how that has been lost. People ignoring each other and losing all form of connection has destroyed the fabric of the place, but my circumstances this morning are a little different. No doubt once I swipe my card and walk through the door, I will still do the right thing. Prior to that, every moment alone with my thoughts is golden.

The main door opens as Jess walks through on her way to the bathroom. I take the opportunity to sneak through, swiping my card to clock-on. 8.55. Thirty-five minutes from the time I left home. Two minutes behind my forecast travel time, which considering the delays, is surprisingly good going.

I may not start working, but I have business to attend to.

CHAPTER 38

8.57AM

'Anthony, wait up.' It is Brooke, who given my plans for the day ahead, is not someone I really wanted to see at this point. 'How was your weekend?'

'I don't understand how time moves at such a different rate when we're not here but it's a proven fact.' This one hadn't sped by for me, but in trying to retain a degree of normality, I used the standard line. I continued towards the fridge to put my lunch in before remembering that I didn't bring anything. The routine is so standard; swipe card, open door, walk to fridge, say good morning, walk to desk. Whenever a step is not required, it still gets followed. It is peak hour for coffee fixes, a queue now forming behind Brooke at the sugar bowl.

'Nine sugars?' I asked Brooke.

'Yeah. Ten makes my coffee too sweet.'

'Shite, I better move. I'm due for Sam's wrath at 9am.'

'Sam's not in. You're spared for today,' Alana, the team support officer tells me.

Since leaving on Friday, my mind has pieced together a plan for today that was all based around the meeting. I had put myself through a mental hell all weekend and now it appeared to be for no reason. I had to work out what direction the plans I had made should now take. I should feel an overwhelming relief from being spared an awkward and painful meeting. Instead I feel the sad reality that I'm probably going to go through all of this mornings angst again tomorrow morning preparing for the same thing. At least I won't have an official locked in time for the meeting and chances are Sam will have other meetings for much of the morning so I could be spared longer. Of course, if I proceed with my plans then tomorrow is removed from the equation. If I wait, I also lose my access to Rob's keys. He's back tomorrow, so my plan can't wait.

Sam is normally the first person in the office each morning. She unlocks her door but leaves her keys in it. I have always intended that the day would come when I would turn the key and leave her locked in that office. Of course, she'd find out who it was but following todays plans it would be too late for her to do anything about it. However insignificant it may seem, it disappointed me to think I'd miss out on that little joy.

I'm always figuratively masked when I'm in the office, and it's on extra tight as I walk towards my desk in the north-western corner of the floor. My mind is trying to process what now to make of the rest of the morning, but I make sure to keep smiling and greeting colleagues as I pass. None of the managers would be so keen seeing me communicating and being friendly with others. Our office has slowly deteriorated from a sociable yet professional environment to one with all the life normally associated with a morgue. Nobody can validate the reasoning for this.

Everything that I've experienced contributes to who I am, and I realise that the same applies, not just to every person, but organisations as well. All the experiences in this workplace have contributed to what it is now. It scares the shit out of me to think about what some of these people have experienced if they think that this is the best form of management. Nobody wants to work here anymore. We struggle to attract good candidates and we struggle to keep good employees. Those that remain are generally too fuelled by anxiety or laziness to make changes to their lives. Some are too incompetent to find something better, but despite the lack of appreciation from above, few fit into that category. There are good people here, but most of them would be so much better in an environment that allowed them to flourish.

Progressive organisations around the world understand that they get the best results out of people when they are comfortable and content. They seek to make employees feel invested in the organisation knowing that this will result in employees giving more. Make them feel satisfied that their labour is making a difference and they will feel valued. Make their environment one where they are appreciated as an individual and they will always give their best. Our management sees any example of people feeling positive in any way and they see it as a sign that those people aren't working their hardest. Treating them mean does not keep them keen.

With Sam not at work, the rest of the management team is out of sight, most likely at the latest crisis meeting that is an essential part of reactive management. There is a slightly more relaxed atmosphere across the floor than we are used to feeling. I feel like the clock has been wound back five years when nothing seemed like such a chore, yet we produced so much more. I turn the computer on and take a deep breath as I survey the scene across the office.

'What are you so happy about Anthony?' asks Ezra, immediately attracting the attention of Bill and Nina who sit across from us.

'I don't know. Life is funny sometimes. I've been dreading this morning because of a meeting I didn't want to have and now that's cancelled. I nearly got myself killed on my bike on the way in, yet finished my ride in a relaxed perfect manner. I left home to what looked and felt the most beautiful autumn day and now half an hour later it's pouring outside. We can't always see what's coming. Change happens fast sometimes.'

'Only so deep I can deal with at 9am Monday morning,' Bill said.

'That's what your girlfriend says.' Ezra was always quick on the lines and we all laughed while Bill searched for a comeback. Beyond our foursome, eyes across the floor remain focused straight ahead, conscious that managers could walk in any moment. This is exactly what I mean. The fun, the banter, it works, yet any of our management team would be in our faces by now if they were around. I'm fortunate to have these guys sitting near me. Most of the staff here have had the life sucked out of them, but Ezra and Bill are excellent value and Nina, though fearful of management, tries to participate a little. No doubt if I was here much longer, the signs of life in the area would see at least one of our group sent to the branches equivalent of Siberia to be replaced by someone well aware of the necessary constraints on personality essential for managerial approval.

I am two different people. Like most people, there is a part of me that lies deep within and very few people ever get to see. There is then the public face. The inner me is dark, while the me that is on display at work is far more extraverted, more entertaining and fun. The strange realisation I'm starting to make is that what I call the masked version of me might be the real person. I think the inner me is the one that has been shaped by the long chain of my history and is a distorted version of who I'm meant to be.

I feel like my nature makes me a people's person. Maybe it is not just a mask that I wear for others, the way it serves so many who are depressed. When I'm smiling and engaged with others, I feel a direct connection to the child running around in the backyard without a care in the world and a head full of dreams. He was happy and he loved being surrounded by people and by happiness. I've often felt like that version of Anthony was killed by abuse, addiction and tragedy. His replacement is the middle-aged me who daily contemplates ending it all.

In these lucid moments I see it differently. The real me wasn't destroyed, just hidden. I hid truths and started becoming different when around others to how I was alone. The problems with addiction never surfaced with anything I did socially. Drinking and gambling in the company of friends never ended up as destructive benders. I stayed in control, well relatively at least. I may throw-up or lose a pay packet, but I collapse in a heap before getting up and moving on. There was no moving on from the state I'd end up in when I was alone. The endings were far more destructive and that's when self-harm became an issue, and the most extreme threats to myself begun to get serious.

When I lost Olivia, I didn't need to be alone, but Cleo and I both felt a connection between grief and solitude that pushed us apart. I can barely remember her presence from the day Olivia died. We shared a house for the next year, yet every vision in my head is of me alone with my despair. For years I believed that Cleo regained functionality in her life quicker than I did because she hadn't experienced as deeper sense of loss as I had. I understand now that this wasn't true. I refused to let anyone in, while with time she gradually let others assist her and share just a small amount of her pain.

I have spent so much of life pushing people away and admittedly much of the reason for this has always been based on my own sense of inadequacy. It hasn't been the belief that people were the problem, but the fear I wasn't worthy of their presence. Alone never felt good, but it was what I knew and what I believed I deserved. Belief is often the enemy of knowledge. No volume of facts can work on their own to conquer harmful beliefs.

I escape to a quiet room under the pretence of making a personal phone call. I need peace to work out what I do now. Everything I'd planned was done with a reason. Proceeding meant part of the point would be lost yet the point was very much secondary. My decision was 40 years in the making and delaying the action based on something peripheral was just delaying the inevitable. If I was choosing to end the pain, waiting longer than necessary defeated the purpose.

So what if I didn't get to give a verbal precursor? I had notes that I would be leaving on my desk. Anyway, I had written a note last time and it turned out pointless. This isn't about anyone understanding, as they're not going to anyway. Plans aren't relevant. It is purely about the result.

The only option was to proceed.

CHAPTER 39

8.59AM

I haven't prepared an explanation that I will use if anyone wonders what I am doing lurking around Rob's desk. To be honest it was unlikely that anyone would ask. I might not belong there, but people in this workplace have a tendency to look at scenarios and ask if it is their business. If the answer is no, then any attempt to get involved meant taking on something more than the already extensive list of responsibilities you had. Nobody wanted to do that, so I assumed I wouldn't need answers.

The northern end of the floor seemed like it was part of a different world, or at least a different department. While the management of our branch was focused on perception, the approach in this branch provided a stark contrast. People here dressed more professionally, they worked more professionally, they were treated more professionally. All of this meant there was no need to try and present an allusion. Staff left the building for a coffee, they chatted around the water cooler, they set their own priorities. They were judged on their overall performance which meant not needing constant measurement of every microscopic task. They were paid to do a job and were left to their own devices to fulfil their responsibilities. Separated by a lunchroom and a short corridor, the distance between branches was either twenty metres or twenty years depending on your choice of measurement.

I made my way across the great divide. While a couple of people acknowledged me, most aimed to avoid the eye contact fearing that my presence was part of the usual hassle of creating more work for someone. Not only was Rob absent, but the woman who sits at the desk next to him wasn't there at that point of time either. I had a fraction more freedom to work in.

Behind his computer was a hook with a key on it. This wasn't the key I needed, but one that unlocked the drawers that housed the master key. Nobody had direct line of vision of me, but I needed discretion when unlocking the drawers. I placed the key in the lock while keeping my head up and my eyes directly on the closest staff members. As much as people wanted to avoid having to deal with me, they weren't going to allow brazen theft of a colleagues personal items without a challenge. I opened the centre drawer a small way then called out across the partition to generate attention and hopefully remove any suspicion.

'Is Rob in today?'

Helen typified exactly what I was dealing with. It seemed like I had forced a major imposition on her day, by asking a question that required the simplest possible response. After the struggle to utter 'No,' her head was down straight away allowing free reign for me to bend slightly and pick up the key I needed. I used my knee to close the drawer and remove the drawer key. I replaced this on the hook and walked away. The minute or so spent at his desk should have been enough to warrant attention but the inherent selfishness of people worked in my favour. I should not be critical, for I can't really claim consistent unselfishness myself. When the phone rings on my desk I do tend to ensure someone else answers through being too 'busy.'

More poignantly to some, my plans for today are what some people consider the ultimate in selfishness. They could not be more wrong though. Without having experienced life in the pit of depression, who can reasonably make judgement. Selfishness would mean that the decision was purely self-centred but that denies a significant part of the motivation. The constant belief for people afflicted in this way, is the burden we are to everyone around us. It feels like there is little more certain than how unselfish it would be to remove ourselves from that role of burden. Sure, people always say that it is not what they would have wanted, but words are cheap. Everyone rallies to show you how valued you are in moments that suit them, but they lack visibility at the most critical times.

Whatever recriminations run through this place, by next week life will continue as it always had before. I will be a memory, replaced in my role by someone new. Someone else will take on the classification as the primary troubled soul of the branch. A few changes will be made to try and support staff's mental health but any attempts for real improvement will be shot down by the argument that my actions had their origins from decades earlier. The time and place of the final moment will be less relevant than the route cause of the problem to management, passing responsibility as always. The costs to productivity of dealing with the issues are burdens they won't want to bare. Never mind the long-term benefits, our management always looks at what sits closest rather than what looms largest.

I shouldn't waste too much thought on what they do. As much as the thoughts verify my attitude towards management, this isn't the time to focus on what is outside my control. I need to get back to my desk to wrap things up.

Passing the kitchen I'm stopped by Reanna, a colleague of mine for the best part of a decade. We've always been a sounding board for each other in our frustrations within these walls. She probably has more reason than me to feel aggrieved in the workplace. While I sit in a higher-level position and have some respect from management, Simone is one of the anonymous faces who they'd really prefer to see gone. She does her job well, but that isn't relevant in Sam's world. She isn't new and she doesn't have the flexibility they want. They blow drawbacks out of the water while I ignoring a whole range of strengths.

'I heard about your big incident Anthony.'

'It hasn't happened yet.'

'No, the fight with fuckface,' she said as if to confirm my thought. I'd always found her to be so mild-mannered, but a frustration that has built at a similar rate to mine has seen this evolve.

'Ah yes, pretty much just means we were in the same place at the same time. That's all it seems to take.'

'No doubt you'll cop more. He can behave how he wants towards any of us but respond at all and management will come down on you.'

'Management don't support him like you think,' I said. She looked to be doubtful of my assertion and reminded me of their decision to promote Terry, but I explained my theory on that. 'They believed the branch was 90% of what they wanted but it was just missing a certain *XYZ*. They were so determined to find someone who excelled at those things that they forgot to look at whether that person could be so destructive in every other way. I think with their time over again things would have been done very differently.'

'You have too much faith in them,' she said while starting to sidle towards a return to her desk.

'No, I just have enough genuine issues with them to avoid casting blame where it isn't warranted.' I smiled and told her to keep her chin up as I walked on with my own chin having to be kept up with the greatest of struggles.

I didn't bother taking a seat when I got back to my desk, just opening my backpack and taking out the two envelopes. The first of these had today's date and the time of 1pm written on it. I assumed that at some point people would interpret what it was and would open it, finding it in a prominent spot on my desk. The other had 'To whom it may concern' on the front and was to stay in my pocket. With that and the key, I was ready. My meeting with Sam may be cancelled, but the more significant meeting of the day was still to proceed. Nobody else needed to attend this one, and I was ready.

CHAPTER 40

9.02 AM

With the key safely secured, I make my way to the door of our branch, forced to run the gauntlet of the open door of Terry's office. Keeping my eyes straight ahead, I knew he would be just as keen to avoid me as I was him. Life often laughs at us in such ways and as I arrived at the door to the branch, he was arriving from the other side.

'Morning Terry. How was your weekend?,' I said, breaking the ice, but avoiding direct eye contact.

'Too quick but all good. Have you got a minute?'

There was no chance any meeting with Terry was ever going to be a minute. Whether we were civil or screaming at each other, the moment I followed him into the office, my plans for the morning were being shaken up. Maybe by the time the conversation I could talk him into taking my place. Perhaps that alone would change my own intention. I need to stop thinking outside of the immediate conversation before I say what's really on my mind.

'I've got to come up with a change to one of the weekly reports,' he said, 'and as you're the guru on these things I was hoping I could get you to have a look at what would work best.'

'Sure,' I said, 'I'm happy to go through anything you've come up with.'

'Well at this stage that's nothing, but I'll have some things in place by this afternoon and I will send them through to you.' He paused briefly before changing topics. 'How are you feeling about Friday?'

'Bit embarrassed. Sometimes you bring out my worst,' I said awkwardly wishing I'd moved just fractionally earlier and avoided this.

'That works both ways.'

'Yeah I know.'

The bizarre dynamic between us was at its finest. Civility. Dare I say, friendliness. It wasn't genuine, yet he acted the role so well that is seemed real. I know that deep within him, there is a similar battle constantly going on as my own. We both understand each others fights, even if we know none of the specifics. In moments like these, we seem to be sharing an empathy built from that, yet it is always just a moment away from an explosive twist, and the completely opposite natures of our respective minds, take over. Whatever was on display, I think we were both processing the thoughts of how much we wish the other one would disappear permanently. Little did he realise that if he hadn't stopped me walking out the door a minute ago, he'd have been a big step closer to his wish.

'When you can't relate to someone at all it's actually not so hard,' Terry said, 'because you don't even attempt to understand their viewpoint. Our problem is that we see the world in a similar way. That leaves us with the false notion that we'll see any given scenario similarly. When we're on the opposite side it becomes more difficult to reconcile why.'

We'd talked enough through the years to know we both had issues with our mental wellbeing, but neither of us had said enough to give any reason to think our struggles were similar. I wondered now if we really were? Had he ever formulated a plot to end it all right here? Had he been abused? Had he lost a child? Whether or not I wanted to admit it, my ultimate workplace rival probably had more in common with me than anyone else I knew. I felt like telling him my plans for the morning to see his reaction and whether he could relate but the potential down sides were too much to come out with something like that. Was Fridays comment a flippant remark or did it have a basis in his own thought process.

'Yeah, that's true' I replied, avoiding saying too much of what I was thinking.

He asked if I'd had a meeting scheduled with Sam today and after telling him the details, he said that he'd had one programmed for this afternoon. He was surprised that we weren't put in the same meeting. He was more relieved than me that Sam wasn't here. My theory of their fragmented relationship was proven to be correct. Our management team had an ability at displaying cohesion on the surface but there were dynamics underneath that at times contrasted this view. It couldn't be more political, with the relationships not too different to what you would see in the halls of parliament.

'Honestly Anthony, there is only so long I will cope in this place,' he said. I never knew how to take this sort of comment. He was a game player, and while his words appeared genuine, they may be serving another motive. Why would he share opinions with someone he distrusts when they could cause him problems? Wouldn't he fear the potential of me using those words against him? If he wanted to say too much about Sam or anyone else I wasn't going to stop him, but neither was I going to create problems by contributing. Whether I would be around to face consequences was irrelevant, I was not going to be part of the problem. Anything he was going to get out of me was going to be about him or me.

'What is your plan?' I asked.

'Keeping my eyes open for opportunities, but what is the point. How different is it going to be anywhere else. Nobody grows up with a dream of working in admin.'

'What did you dream of?'

'Various unrealistic things,' he said. 'At this point of life, I prefer to stick to realism.'

'I wouldn't. Reality is what makes people like me jump off buildings.' The words came out without me even realising. I hoped that he interpreted it as a response to his statement from Friday rather than my own mindset.

His look intensified. 'Unless they've been small buildings, I'm fairly sure you haven't.'

'Well, the day is young.' I smiled as I said it, to lighten the mood and add more credence to the idea that I was merely playing with words. He must have taken it this way, returning to talking about himself.

'I do think about a whole career change but the only way I don't go backwards salary wise is to study and that's going to write off a couple of years. Given the age of my kids, that is something I don't want to do.'

'My dad used to grow roses,' I said. 'They were stunning, but only courtesy of the foul-smelling fertiliser he used. The beautiful results in life usually require wading through shit on the journey. You can't just choose the best destination, you need to decide what shit you can cope with on the way.'

'And after all your years here you're willing to put up with the stench in this office?'

'I'm not so willing to put up with the stench in my life. The air I breathe seems no fresher when I get outside.' I paused for a moment, thinking it was the perfect segue. 'I shall at least give that idea a bit of a try,' angling to the door of the office.

'You're not always uplifting Anthony, but always thought provoking.'

As I turned to walk away, he stopped me again.

'Anthony, who's the enemy?'

'What?'

'There is so much politics in this office. There are alliances. There are enemies. You trust the wrong people and they fuck you over. I think at times you're too busy making major issues out of minor conflicts and not seeing where the real problems are. You aren't the enemy for me, and if you think I am for you, then you're missing something.'

'We're allies?'

'No, but we should be. We're both getting screwed by the same sociopath.'

Even as I listened to him describe Sam contemptuously, I still wondered what his end game was and where he thought I fit in. Terry drives much of the politics that he refers to. He was always going to look for an opportunity to screw over anyone he doesn't like, most notably me. Sam is on a different scale, but although she may be more of an issue, she was fighting bigger targets than us.

'There are that many complaints that had to be investigated on her that never ended up happening,' Terry said. 'There's only one reason for that. She is being protected by someone powerful. They're not doing that for her sake, they only do that for themselves. She's got dirt on people at the absolute highest level and she is using that as her insurance policy. Run this place on the verge of criminal negligence. Bully people, no problems. Promote incompetence, sure. Nothing stops her.'

'You say it as though it's a revelation,' I said. 'I took it for granted sometime ago, I just learnt it wasn't my fight.'

'So why am I your fight?' he asked.

'You're not. My only fight is within. Maybe I swing too hard and you're close enough to get hit.' It wasn't completely true. He had been the cause of many fights, but this wasn't the time for accuracy. I made the move out of his office and took the few steps towards the door that exited our branch, walking quickly to the elevators. I thought I heard his voice as I turned the corner, but didn't want to be held up. He always had something else to add, and a minute could easily turn into fifteen. For someone who would fire a staff member for wasting time, he didn't mind doing it himself. He always found ways of arguing points that justified behaviour in himself that he would admonish in others. This hypocrisy infuriated me, though he was in the right place for that.

In theory I had all the time in the world, but my mind had reached a point while talking to Terry that it felt like it was now or never. I was committed to now.

CHAPTER 41

9.10AM

I paused for a few moments before unlocking the door. What the fuck was I doing? I've long believed that there was always an air of inevitability to the end of my road, but this time and place should not be it. If the act was to be a conclusion, it should provide some context to the story that preceded it. Terry was insignificant. An arsehole, sure, but not a major factor that was relevant to this moment. I hate my job, but I hate it in the same way I hate broccoli or reality television, not in the way I hate SIDS, paedophiles or cancer. The letter in my pocket would provide an explanation but it didn't do the event justice. What would?

I found a suitable spot to sit and appreciated the light, misty rain now falling on my head. The refreshing feeling in the open air 40 metres above the ground had me feeling somewhat opposite to what it was that had brought me here. If I'd been able, I would have come here in years gone by for my smoke breaks with Ezra. God, I wish I had a cigarette with me now. It's been a long time, but here and now the idea seems like perfection.

I didn't want to be here. I didn't want to do this. If I did, surely I'd have gone straight to the ledge and jumped, yet here I was just sitting in the rain. The raindrops blending in with the teardrops. It wasn't about wants. I had to do it this time.

'Anthony.' Terry hadn't finished our conversation after all, so he'd followed me up here. I hadn't locked the door behind me, so he was able to come straight through. 'What the hell are you doing up here?'

'What you told me to do on Friday.'

'For fuck's sake. When have you ever done anything I said? I'm sorry, it was a flippant remark. Didn't I explain that downstairs.'

I couldn't look him in the eyes, but I nodded gingerly.

'It's not about you,' I said. I hated having him see me like this. 'Why did you follow me?'

'You and I are very much alike, whether you want to believe it or not. 75% of people who attempt, have talked about it in advance, even if only minimally. I figured the remarks you made to me may be the only things you had said. It could have meant that I was the only person able to react.'

'I would have thought you'd be the one person in this place who might understand.'

'Depends what you mean by understand,' he said. 'The self-hatred I get. The desire to escape it all makes sense. Acting upon it, no. That I don't understand.'

'How can you just accept this endlessly? Even when any prospect of hope is gone?'

'I have to,' he said. 'Whatever it takes, we have to for those around us.'

'I don't have anyone.'

'Buy a dog. If that isn't enough take your head out of your arse and see who you do have. You don't need to have a spouse or children or whatever it is that you feel is missing, that others might have. You might want that, envy that or whatever but we all have our own situation to deal with and you make the best of it.'

The amount of anger and frustration that this man had made me feel over the years, and now it was him that was as the source of salvation that may keep me alive. I knew he was right, but that was depressing. I told him that I wanted to make a difference to people.

'Making a difference in the lives of other people isn't always what you think. Maybe your custom is the difference between a small business owner surviving or failing. Maybe your influence gets someone to read a book that changes their life and in doing so they then change the lives of others. Maybe the bitterness you hold towards an enemy helps change them for the better,' he said looking at me more poignantly, 'so that the lives of people around them improve. Without noticing it, you are constantly making a significant difference to other people.'

'I need someone to make a significant difference to me too,' I replied despite feeling selfish in saying it.

'Fair enough, but how do you make that happen. Nothing falls in your lap. Whatever you seek, you need to evaluate ways of finding it and making it happen. The action you choose to take or avoid will dictate the results.'

'My child died at 11 months. That wasn't what I did or didn't do.'

'No.' I thought he couldn't answer me, but his pause was only momentary. 'After years of grieving as was appropriate, there also needed to be attempts at building something new. You deserved something good in return for what happened but that's not how it works. You only get something good by going after it, not by sitting back just because you deserve it.'

I had contemplated suicide many times in life, but today was the second time I had reached the point of taking the steps towards the ultimate action. On these two occasions I had been met with the words of two people who I considered part of my problem, not part of my solution, in Cleo and Terry. Previously the only thing I'd have considered they would have in common was general contempt for me.

'I checked into a hotel one day planning to jump off the balcony. I ended up taking a phone call from my ex-wife, probably the last person who could have talked me around but she did. Now you.'

'Clearly we both need you. Maybe in my case it's to make your life hell so that I can feel better about myself.'

'That's no way to live.'

'Long term it's not, but there are times when you've got to revert to the *whatever it takes* approach to get through the short term.'

Terry's emotions always seemed to be close to the edge. In front of me, the only thing he would release was anger, but I remember Madeleine referring to him as a mess on multiple occasions. I could see emotion welling within him now.

'My brother committed suicide 16 years ago. It destroyed all of us and from that day on. However far I've sunk, life has always been built around the principle of whatever it takes.'

'I'm sorry,' I offered both as a tribute for his loss and for drawing him into the confronting scene of my trauma.

'You understand my passion on the topic?'

I nodded. There were so many things I couldn't understand about his approach through aspects of life that seemed to contradict the mindset he had here. Such determination to protect others from the ultimate attack of mental illness yet so willing to provoke mental illness with his combative approach made no sense to me. For now, there were more important things than trying to understand Terry.

'Why did you want to do this at work?'

Surely he knew that he was half of the reason. He would have appreciated that Sam was the other half, but getting too deeply into reasons wasn't what I wanted at this stage. I decided instead to use a famous music reference and told him that it was because I don't like Mondays.

'You know the story behind that song, right? I guess at least your plans weren't that bad,' he said. 'Though not much better. Come downstairs with me. Let's get a coffee.'

I told him that I was surprised he cared enough to follow me. He said that he was too concerned about how much paperwork he'd have had to deal with if he'd let me go through with it. His delivery was deadpan, and I wasn't sure how much of a factor this was. Knowing our practices and procedures, he wasn't wrong about what would be involved, but I'd like to think there was something a little more human to his motivations.

I was surprised that his first thought wasn't reporting all that had happened to create trouble for me, but I guess we'd shared enough at this point of time to have built a bond. My faith in him was far from set in stone, but I was willing to follow his lead at this point.

We made our way to the door which I locked behind me. He asked about the key and I told him that I had lifted it from Rob's desk. As soon as I did, I realised how much my guard was down. This was still Terry. Telling him more than I needed could still come back to bite me. He told me he needed to go back to his office first to get his wallet but once we were back on the floor he took me around via the far entrance. We went straight into Madeleine's office and I realised the coffee wouldn't be happening. I guess there was no point fighting what I knew had to follow.

My head on my hands which were crossed on Madeleine's desk. I couldn't look up and make eye contact with anyone. Moisture welled in my eyes without turning into ongoing tears. Terry asked me if it was alright if he told Madeleine everything. I knew that saying no was futile, and better Madeleine than anyone else. Once he finished, he whispered something else to her, which I suspected may be about contacting some of the essential people in the situation; security, employee assistance, the emergency services, my personal contact and Sam.

Terry then left me with Madeleine and it was time to try and explain things again. The brief relief that came in the moment Terry talked me to safety was over. The reality was sinking in. Every negative that had driven me to this point still existed, but now there was one extra issue on top of it. The workplace now knew the real me.

Madeleine was crying. Apologising, though there wasn't a thing she had done in seven years that warranted an apology.

As always, she was ready and willing to do anything required. Consequences never allowed her to deviate from the principle that in every workplace, people must always come first.

Would I ever be able to work here again? Despite the change of plans, my belief that this would be my last ever day here would surely still prove true.

CHAPTER 42

9.24am

Two security guards and a medical officer arrived on the floor and took me downstairs. As we left, I turned back to Terry and asked when he was buying me that coffee.

'That's what you're focussed on now?' he replied.

'More about how genuine your words were,' I said.

'Well I never did say that I was buying, so you do go adding your interpretation to my words.'

I must have given him a quizzical look as he explained that he asked me to join him for a coffee, not that he'd buy it. In the scheme of things such semantics may seem irrelevant, but considering the fight that pushed todays action had stemmed from such a misinterpretation, there was a poignancy to it. Another reminder that what one person says and another person hears are not always the same. Whether or not he realised it, Terry was now making my point for me.

'Everything I said to stop you was genuine,' he added.

I wonder. As the only witness to what happened on the roof, how will this story play out when people hear it? Is this going to be the heroic tale of Terry saving my life through his understanding and care? The thought of that was nauseating. I appreciate what he did and said, but it wasn't heroism. The scene would never have occurred, at least not here and now, if not for his words and actions. If a firefighter commits arson, and is then on the scene conquering the fire, he can't be called a hero. That may overstate Terry's role in getting me on the roof, but less than I fear he will overstate his role in getting me back down.

The standard darkness of an intense depressive mood can get enveloped by an even greater blackness following a trigger. At that point, there is no ability to think through anything with rationale. I have experienced this many times over, and I know that when I am at that point, there is no limit to what can happen. Ongoing depression is debilitating, but it takes a trigger to reach that next step, however briefly it holds.

Terry can trigger me, but today when our paths first crossed he was unusually conciliatory. Sam's more subtle nature less frequently sets me off, but the planned meeting for today had an agenda that was guaranteed to pull my trigger. I know what I was going to say. I know what her response would have been. I know the blackness that would have taken over as I walked out, got in that elevator, opened the door and walked straight to the ledge without a pause for thought.

Thought doesn't happen in that mode. I never wanted things to end that way. Nobody ever does. We open our mouths to scream for help, but we're incapable of making a sound. Today I was heard, but it will take time before I know whether that is a good thing.

What consequences awaited me was a mystery. Last time I was at this point, nobody other than Cleo ever knew. She was far enough away to be unable to do anything. She accepted my assurances that I was safe. She followed up consistently in the short term so she could be certain that remained the case. Nothing more happened and nothing more was needed. Now the authorities were involved. Between police and mental health experts, this would be handled under the most official means. What the outcome would be regarding my employment was something that I would only discover with time. I doubted I would ever be walking through this office again. For now, none of that really mattered.

I knew I would be institutionalised for some period. The provision of resources for mental health in our society is insufficient, so I was unlikely to get the level of care that I probably needed. I knew I needed protection from myself for a while. There was a big rebuild needed in my life, and I needed a huge amount of help to begin that.

For most of my colleagues it was not yet morning teatime. The topic of gossip for today was obvious. They would be oblivious to what had happened, but they would have seen Terry, Madeleine and Patrick in various states of panic. They'd know something was going on, and it would not take long before word spilt of what it had been. From there, it will quickly be universal knowledge.

A little more than an hour ago I was still home. Yes, I had every minute planned. They didn't quite all work out that way. Sure enough, my plan didn't involve Sam failing to be at work today, nor did it involve the interruptions from Terry, both in his office and on the roof. How typical it is that the two people who have made life hell in here would stand in my way, even if it was actually for the best.

This morning feels like half a lifetime. My mind habitually replays moments from across my life, but never quite so many, so quickly as it did on the ride to work this morning. Life supposedly flashes before your eyes in the instant before death. The proximity wasn't that close, yet the experience wasn't too dissimilar to what people talk of. My loves, my losses, my triumphs and tragedies. The good times and the terror. I saw them all. Don't people normally see that and wish to hang on? I didn't.

I hope that the time will come when I can look back at today with gratitude that it ended as it did. The very fact that I can acknowledge a hope is a starting point. Hope had been lost some time ago. However small it may now be, I had something to cling to. I knew more existed, and maybe day by day it would all start getting closer.

Everyone has their own stories. Those I share an office with will use my descent as a momentary distraction from their lives, but before long today will simply file into their distant memories. Forty years on maybe Terry will reminisce with his grandchildren about the day he saved a life. Maybe he and I will be the only people who remember it. Things that seem huge to everyone at the time, eventually disappear into insignificance for those a step removed from the event.

How does a person feel in this position? A second chance at life so frequently becomes a blessing, but not at this point. Nobody makes this decision without being at the ultimate point of desperation. Although I willingly stood aside thanks to the words of my nemesis, the desperation that saw me on the roof did not disappear with those words. If anything I was now subjected to an even greater low. Not only had I failed at being able to live a reasonable life, I'd failed at being able to plan a suitable end.

Half an hour ago I was talking to colleagues who liked me. Well, not the real me, but a version that I'd played along to. Maybe the best of them always saw through the mask and always knew there was a little more to me. I don't expect it, but I cannot rule out the chance that those few people may not give up on me. That will be a bonus, but it is irrelevant unless I can stop giving up on myself.

Terry's words were vastly different to Cleo's two years ago, but the impact was similar. Both people were able to find a way of reaching through to me when I doubted anything could. They both, for whatever timeframe, were able to quell the desire that was overpowering me, to bring all of my issues to an end. I knew that they had not fuelled any great desire to live, but that was something that I would need to find for myself. Turning life around was a journey of many steps. For people who I'd considered as being against me, to help me on the first steps was more than I could hope for. The steps I take for myself will dictate whether anything changes.

The pit that I have felt myself disappearing in was dug through the events of my life that all had their origin in people. It was Olivia, the person I loved most and Stuart, the person I despised. People shape us, both the good and the bad, the loved and the hated. Every person can shape us in some small way. Even the people I ride past and invent stories about have had an impact. The stories don't need to be real to have power, nor the people. At times they have provided me with an outlet that has brought a smile to my face or provided a little more understanding of how the differences in people can enrich us all.

In a quiet room I wait with the security guards and the medical officer. She is massively underprepared to deal with something like this, and I'm sure was hoping her next call would be the application of a band-aid or dispensing a head-ache tablet. She seems more fearful of saying or doing something wrong than Terry, Madeleine and Patrick did when initially faced with my situation. They know the danger is over for now. There calmness, at least on the surface, was admirable. Terry has probably disappeared now to add a description of his self-proclaimed heroism to his resume. I shouldn't care.

Thinking back on the people I passed on the way to work this morning, I wonder how accurate the pictures I painted of their lives were. Was it just another day at work for each of them? I'm sure that some of them will have had a moment or two that stood out and would remain memorable for a long time to come, yet I was equally as certain that none would have experienced a day anything like mine. Maybe one of them may have been a people watcher, and on noticing me ride past, may have made up a story for my day. Even the most vivid imagination could not have created something to match my reality.

One day I will make the same journey that has been so familiar for all these years. I will see some of the same faces and create new identities for others. Even if I do not have a destination, I only need a pathway to start. People may have led me into the dark, but sometimes the remedy to a problem isn't so far removed from the cause. I believed I did not need anyone else. I always did and I always will.

I only bought my new bike a week ago. I wonder what will happen to it. If I'm never allowed back here will someone get it home for me? How crazy it is that in the scheme of todays events, I can be focussed on a detail like that. So close to the fine line between life and death, yet I am only ever moments away from switching focus to the insignificant details that most people would never consider. I've never been good at letting go.

Brought back from the precipice, I don't feel a sense of relief, but neither do I carry disappointment. Right now, there is just life. Everything within it is merely perspective.

ACKNOWLEDGEMENTS

Writing a book can feel like a lonely and individual process, but it's not a solo act. Without the support, encouragement and advice of others, the ideas remain in the head.

The concept of a novel set entirely on the bicycle commute to work first came to me twenty years ago. From time to time in the ensuing years, ideas would come into my head about how to turn that concept into something more substantial. Of course, I wasn't a writer and the idea that I ever would be seemed unrealistic.

With the right advice and encouragement, I finally saw a way of bringing this all together. Two decades of thoughts and ideas turned into a first draft that was written in six weeks. It was only after completing a full draft that I understood what the story should be. The subsequent rewrite saw a new protagonist, a more connected story and a clearer expression of the message. Every life is a story. It twists, it turns, but every part of it links together. Yesterday's crises will in time be just a memory, but it will leave an imprint within us that plays a role in shaping us today and directing our tomorrow.

There are difficult elements to this story that can make it a challenging read in the same way that it was challenging to write. I am glad it is that way, for the great rewards in life stem from the greatest challenges. For someone who has been focusing on holiday fiction, this is a far deeper and more confronting style of novel. My desire to be a writer was never to make routine choices, but to tell stories that would have an impact. I hope that people who read this book are reminded that the people they interact with each day are living their own story, often filled with traumas they mightn't show. Empathy, tolerance and understanding can change lives.

I used to ride to work every day. I worked in the public sector in an office in the CBD. I am a similar age to Anthony. From this, people may think that I am telling my story. This is most certainly not the case. Anthony goes through a dozen or more traumas from the course of his life, ranging from the loss of his house in the Ash Wednesday fires of 1980 to recent heart surgery. Some of these moments are drawn from personal experience, while many are not. I could see the character of Anthony as a young child like me, and the man at 9am on the 16th May who was so different. The character couldn't reach such a different end point to mine without having ridden a different journey.

My deepest love and thanks go to my wife Alison. Quite simply, this book would never have been written without you. Not only did you design and create the cover as well as providing ideas and opinions in the midst of my struggles, you have brought me a happiness that allows me to examine life in a way sufficient to capture it through words. You laugh when you see me get so emotional over silly things, but emotion is the essence of life. A story only impacts people if it can capture an emotional connection between character and reader. A writer can only capture the necessary emotion to achieve this by understanding it. Any ability I have to do this stems from the depth of emotion you've uncovered within me.

To my family; Pat, Leonie, Hella, and the dear departed Robert, Marty and Ollie. My gratitude for your love and support is eternal. I wouldn't be who I am without the influence that each of you have had on me. I'm sure none of you could have foreseen this direction for me, but the influence that you each had has contributed enormously to enabling this.

To the friends who may see people, places or events that might stir memories particularly Simon, Mark, Michael, Lisa, Kat, Tania and Sam. Thankyou for those moments and for the friendships that led to them.

To the colleagues who worked in one of the various offices I spent twenty or so years working in. So many of you made turning up and dealing with the not so good parts of the workplace seem so much easier. We all remember times that were challenging and draining, but my strongest memories are of the laughs, the friendships and the unity that so many of us shared. Thankfully, my experiences are far different to that which Anthony Speed knew, and it wouldn't have been this way without such great people. I particularly thank Kasia, Mel and Michelle who at various times in the past twenty years have gone beyond the call of colleagues.

To see an idea that has festered for so long finally make it into print fills me with pride, but furthermore, it has me determined to continue down this path. The next books will be very different, yet there still is that similar connection through an intense focus on the human condition. In each of those, the setting will be as significant as the characters. I hope you will join me on each of those journeys.

ABOUT THE AUTHOR

A business graduate from the University of South Australia, C.R. Page had never contemplated a career in writing until the passion was spiked by a series of major life events. Through several funerals and his own wedding, he wrote eulogies, vows and speeches that earned sufficient recognition for him to take his hobby further. He was a prize winner in the Campbelltown Literary Awards in 2020 for his short story 'One Person at a Time.' He won the major prize at the Living Landscape Writers Festival in 2022 for his short story 'Sanctuary'.

In 2022 he launched the website crpage.com.au writing blog posts on a range of issues as they relate to the range of travel-inspired novels he is planning to release from late 2022.

'The Ride to Work' is the debut novel for C.R. Page.